LEAVE NO STONE UNTURNED

W9-BYF-394

A LEXIE STARR MYSTERY NOVEL

LEAVE NO STONE UNTURNED

JEANNE GLIDEWELL

FIVE STAR
A part of Gale, Cengage Learning

Margaret E. Heggan Free Public Library
208 East Holly Avenue
Hurffville, New Jersey 08080

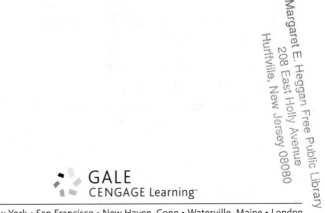

GALE
CENGAGE Learning

Detroit • New York • San Francisco • New Haven, Conn • Waterville, Maine • London

GALE
CENGAGE Learning·

Copyright © 2008 by Jeanne Glidewell.

A Lexie Starr Series.

Five Star Publishing, a part of Gale, Cengage Learning.

ALL RIGHTS RESERVED

This novel is a work of fiction. Names, characters, places and incidents are either the product of the author's imagination, or, if real, used fictitiously.

No part of this work covered by the copyright herein may be reproduced, transmitted, stored, or used in any form or by any means graphic, electronic, or mechanical, including but not limited to photocopying, recording, scanning, digitizing, taping, Web distribution, information networks, or information storage and retrieval systems, except as permitted under Section 107 or 108 of the 1976 United States Copyright Act, without the prior written permission of the publisher.

The publisher bears no responsibility for the quality of information provided through author or third-party web sites and does not have any control over, nor assume any responsibility for, information contained in these sites. Providing these sites should not be construed as an endorsement or approval by the publisher of these organizations or of the positions they may take on various issues.

Set in 11 pt. Plantin

Printed on permanent paper.

LIBRARY OF CONGRESS CATALOGING-IN-PUBLICATION DATA

Glidewell, Jeanne.
  Leave no stone unturned / Jeanne Glidewell. — 1st ed.
    p. cm.
  "A Lexie Starr Mystery Novel."
  ISBN-13: 978-1-59414-649-7 (hardcover : alk. paper)
  ISBN-10: 1-59414-649-7 (hardcover : alk. paper)
  1. Middle-aged women—Fiction. 2. Mothers and daughters—Fiction. 3. Domestic fiction. I. Title.
PS3607.L57L43 2008
813'.6—dc22   2007047651

First Edition. First Printing: May 2008.

Published in 2008 in conjunction with Tekno Books and Ed Gorman.

Printed in the United States of America
1 2 3 4 5 6 7 12 11 10 09 08

For my father, Joseph Van Sittert,
and my mother-in-law, Ruth Glidewell,
whom I both loved dearly
and will miss every day of my life.

ACKNOWLEDGMENTS

I'd like to thank my wonderful agent, Mike Valentino, of Cambridge Literary Associates; my dear and talented editor, Alice Duncan; and Five Star Publishing, for their faith in me. I'd also like to offer my sincere gratitude to my friend and fellow author, Evelyn Horan, for her help and guidance, as well as my mother, Carol Van Sittert, my sister, Sarah Goodman, and my beloved husband, Bob Glidewell, for their love and support. It was Sarah who encouraged me, and convinced me I should write a cozy mystery series, and Bob who, through sickness and in health, has stood beside me every step of the way throughout our blessed marriage.

ONE

Should I warn my daughter her husband could be a murderer, or go home and file my nails while I sip on a cup of strong coffee? Coffee sounded tempting, but it'd have to wait, I decided, as I pulled into Wendy's driveway on the way home from the library. My son-in-law, Clay, was in the front yard talking to a couple of friends he'd met at a gym he'd joined when he first moved here. Clay and Wendy had just returned from a week's vacation in the Colorado Rockies. It'd been a belated honeymoon.

It was unseasonably, almost unbelievably, cool for early October. I could see Clay's breath as he spoke. He was telling a story with his hands, making large, sweeping motions that held his friends in rapt attention, their eyes open wide and transfixed. As I watched, Clay aimed an invisible gun at the mailbox and fired, apparently killing the mailbox immediately. His friends high-fived him, showing admiration for his aim and skill. The gesture sent chills up my spine and made the hair on the back of my neck stand on end like a cat who'd just seen its reflection in a mirror.

It was then I noticed in Clay's truck bed a very large, very dead, bull moose with an immense span of antlers and the customary large hump on its nose. Its chin was propped up on the tailgate, its eyes open, its tongue lolling out the right side of its mouth. Couldn't someone have showed a little respect and closed its eyelids? Being stared at by a dead moose was giving me the willies.

For a moment, I wondered if the animal was poached, or bagged legally. Then I realized that you couldn't just prop a poached moose up in the bed of your truck and drive four hundred miles down I-70. I felt sad for the animal, though, and sad for its family and friends. I also felt sorry for anyone who'd been following the truck from Colorado with a dead moose staring down into his windshield. It would have made it difficult to concentrate on driving.

The front door of the house was open, so I walked into the foyer. My daughter was on the phone, speaking with a taxidermist. The Yellow Pages, lying open on the counter, showed an ad that claimed, "You bang 'em, we'll hang 'em."

"Okay, okay—okay, okay—okay," Wendy said into the mouthpiece. She sounded like Joe Pesci in the *Lethal Weapon* movies.

"Okay, okay—okay."

Shouldn't Wendy have taken more time with her answers? I wondered. She was making important—well, at least, permanent—decisions. That moose would most likely be looking one way or the other for the rest of its dead life. I glanced beyond the foyer into their family room. The massive moose head would have to hang from the stone fireplace, which rose up toward the vaulted ceiling. To have him staring straight ahead would be eerie, almost threatening. He should be mounted so he was looking left into the room. Why would a dead moose walk into a perfectly well-decorated room and look the other way? Martha Stewart would be appalled at the very idea.

Of course, I thought, if he looked the other way, he'd be looking directly into the kitchen. And that made sense in an odd way too. Moose are huge animals. They must be hungry a lot of the time.

Oh, good grief. What was I thinking? My recent discoveries

were impairing my ability to think rationally. I really did need a stiff cup of espresso, laced liberally with Kahlúa. I didn't imbibe often, but I could use a drink right then, for medicinal purposes.

I glanced around at the other family room walls and noticed for the first time a number of animal heads. There were no full body mounts, just heads with fixed eyes staring into the room. Wendy and Clay had lived in the house a month, moving in just after their August eighteenth wedding. I'd hesitated to bother the newlyweds during the first few weeks of their marriage, so I'd diligently kept my distance.

Wendy and Clay are both outdoorsy, and apparently Clay is a hunter, as well. I couldn't visualize Wendy shooting a moose. She'd always had a hard time stepping on a spider. Although she'd probably feel right at home in the middle of a forest, I couldn't quite imagine her feeling comfortable in her own family room, surrounded by all these dead, mounted animals. Maybe I didn't know my daughter as well as I thought.

"Okay, okay. Yeah, that's fine—okay," I heard Wendy saying. She looked at me and smiled. It was the dreamy smile of a woman in love. My stomach churned.

What I now suspected about Clay scared me half to death and made me almost nauseated. Suddenly I just wanted to go back to my own little house and think about it a while longer. I wanted to prop my feet up in my own little family room with no accusatory eyes staring down from the walls of the room. I wanted to sip at that cup of coffee and Kahlúa. I was no longer sure I should tell Wendy what I'd come to tell her. I decided I needed to contemplate the potential consequences of that decision further before I acted on it. An unwise, hasty decision could produce devastating results. I was concerned about her safety more than anything, but didn't want to upset her with my unconfirmed suspicions either.

I jotted down a note on a pad of paper from the hall table.

"Call you later," I wrote. Wendy glanced at my note and nodded. I hurried back to my car, waved briefly at Clay and his friends, backed out of the driveway, and headed south before Clay had an opportunity to walk over and speak to me. I couldn't risk talking to him right now. I knew my voice would sound anxious and unnatural because I'd just discovered there was a good possibility Clay had murdered his first wife, Eliza, over two years ago. I was fairly sure my daughter had no idea Clay had been married before, or that Eliza had ever existed, and I was suddenly not convinced it'd be in her, or my, best interest for her to be informed of what I'd just learned.

After all, I was quite certain Wendy was aware of my skepticism about my new son-in-law, as hard as I tried to hide my aversion to Clay. I realized part of my animosity might stem from jealousy, for I was no longer the most important person in Wendy's life. But mostly it was an uneasiness I felt around him, as if Clay wasn't being entirely open with either of us.

Wendy had accused me of trying to control her and how she chose to live her life on several occasions, so I was very hesitant to say anything negative about Clay now. She might not be too quick to forgive my interference in her new marriage. Should I risk her disdain, or should I first try to find out more of the details in case the first wife had not been killed, as the authorities suspected, but had eventually turned up safe and sound at a friend's house and the marriage had dissolved naturally? Perhaps I'd even discover the Clay Pitt in question really didn't have a thing to do with Wendy's husband.

I didn't often have to make such a critical decision, and I was afraid I'd make the wrong one and endanger the close relationship I shared with my only child. And that was the last thing I wanted to do.

Two

My name is Alexandria. Alexandria Marie Starr, or Lexie to my family and friends. I'm forty-eight, and at that pre-geriatric age where I'm too young for my senior citizen's discount, but knee-deep into middle age. I need one pair of glasses for distance, another pair for reading, and have learned not to be too concerned about the clarity of anything in between.

I have thick, curly brown hair with lighter highlights, compliments of a local beauty salon. It's a constant three-month cycle of cut, trim, trim, perm, highlight; cut, trim, trim, perm, highlight. During the three-month cycle there is a span of about four and a half days that my hair, with no fuss or bother, looks exactly like I want it to. The rest of the time my hairstyle resembles either a French poodle or that of a heroin addict in a mug shot. But for four and a half days every season I look pretty hot. Well, luke-warm anyway.

I stand a shade under five feet, two inches tall, and weigh between 120 and 140, depending on the season. During the summer, when my garden is producing and I'm eating lots of veggies, I weigh in at about 120. During the winter, when I'm forced to substitute chocolate chip cookie dough ice cream for asparagus and squash, my weight drifts up toward 140. Fortunately, I have a good-sized walk-in closet that accommodates small, medium, and large wardrobes.

Circumstances have required me to be independent and self-reliant. I've had to be both mother and father to Wendy since

Margaret E. Heggan Free Public Library
208 East Holly Avenue
Hurffville, New Jersey 08080

she was seven years old. That was the year her father, Chester, died from an embolism. As they say, he never knew what hit him. We'd taken Wendy to the theater to see a Disney movie one night and had just returned to the house. Chester walked in the door and fell to the floor. My husband was dead before his head touched the carpet. That was the moment my life, and Wendy's life, changed forever. It was suddenly the two of us against the world. Fortunately for me, Wendy's a loving daughter, and our personalities are complementary. Throughout the years, we've always been close.

In the years following Chester's death, I tried to give Wendy all the advantages a child with both parents might enjoy. I wanted her to experience as much as possible so she'd be a well-rounded individual. I wanted her to go to interesting places and to do exciting things. I thought such adventures could only enhance her confidence and self-esteem.

When Wendy was ten I took her to Disneyland. I bought her a cheap charm bracelet there, so she could collect charms from the different places I took her in the years to follow. "It's to show where you've been," I told her. By the time she was eighteen, a gold-plated version, and then a ten-carat version, had replaced it. Finally a twenty-four-carat gold bracelet graced her wrist. It was my gift to her on her twenty-first birthday.

The bracelet held many charms. Among others, there was one shaped like the Space Needle from our visit to Seattle, a peach-shaped charm that had "Georgia" etched across it, a miniature of South Dakota's Mount Rushmore, and an Eiffel Tower replica from our trip to Paris. Wendy was proud of each charm and the memories they evoked. The charms showed all the places she'd been. She wore the bracelet everywhere, even to bed much of the time.

The two of us got by pretty well during those years. Chester had left me with what would turn out to be several wise investments, and also a substantial insurance policy. I wanted the money to last me through the "golden" years, so I was never extravagant. But I was never cheap either. I'd scrimp on the trivial things so that I could afford to splurge on the important things. I never wanted my daughter to be humiliated by showing up at a school dance in a dress she wasn't proud to be seen wearing.

Throughout Wendy's teenage years I unfailingly put a hundred dollars a week into a college fund. After her high school graduation she left Shawnee, Kansas, and went east to Massachusetts to go to medical school, eventually settling on a career in pathology. After returning to Kansas, she was quickly offered a position as an assistant to the county coroner. To earn her living, she'd perform autopsies to search for the cause of death. I had hoped she'd become a pediatrician.

"I get too emotionally attached to the patients. I can't handle it when medical technology can't save them and they die, despite our best efforts," she told me when I asked why she'd chosen working with deceased patients rather than live ones.

"But now all of your patients are dead!" I replied. "Every single one of them!"

"Yes, I know. But I'll never have known them as living, breathing human beings with at least a sliver of hope to survive. There's no opportunity to become close to them. It's difficult to become attached to a cadaver, Mom, trust me. Once a stiff, always a stiff."

"So I guess 'bedside manner' is not a big concern in your chosen field?" I asked, rather sarcastically. I didn't appreciate her lack of compassion. I hadn't raised her to be so callous and insensitive.

"No, I guess not, and that's another advantage of this field. I can dance naked around my customers while telling offensive jokes, and it doesn't seem to bother them a bit." She saw the look of horror on my face and jabbed my shoulder playfully. "I'm kidding. You know I'd never do that. Lighten up. I do have to be considerate of the survivors' feelings. I take pride in being able to offer comfort to them at their time of loss."

I was relieved by my daughter's last remarks. She'd been such a softhearted, gentle little girl. I would regret seeing her adopt a dispassionate attitude now. It was difficult enough to accept the thought of my only child choosing such a depressing, gruesome occupation. But I realized I had to let her make her own decisions. I prayed the consequences of some of her decisions wouldn't be too harsh. And perhaps she'd have to develop that kind of hardened attitude not to be emotionally ravaged by every "stiff" that passed through her office. I can remember attending tearful funerals Wendy had staged as a child. I would try to console her while she sobbed over a dead butterfly, or field mouse, as she buried it in our backyard.

One day, during her final year in medical school, Wendy called. "I have good news and bad news for you, Mom. Which would you like to hear first?"

After I told her I'd rather get the bad news over with first, she told me she'd lost her golden charm bracelet. She'd looked everywhere, searched her dorm room from top to bottom, scoured every place she could remember being, and it was just nowhere to be found. She was devastated about it, and so was I.

"Now how will anyone know where I've been?" she asked me over the phone, with an odd mixture of sadness and laughter in her voice. She was choked up and sounded as if she were on the verge of tears. Like me, Wendy often laughed to keep from crying. I was keenly aware of how sentimental Wendy was about the bracelet, so I vowed to myself that I'd replace the bracelet and as many of the charms as I could. It would make a wonderful Christmas present later on.

Then Wendy's tone brightened considerably as she told me

she'd also met the man she was going to marry. She'd actually first met him about a year ago in a trendy little coffee shop on campus called Java Joe's. They'd visited over a cup of coffee occasionally in the following months, but had been officially dating for only a few weeks. Wendy declared he was everything she'd ever wanted in a husband. He didn't know it yet, she said, but she was going to make him see he couldn't live without her.

He was a few years older than Wendy, and after taking a hiatus following a four-year stint in the Navy, to work in one dead-end job after another, he'd eventually returned to college to pursue a degree in criminology. He stayed with a friend in Boston during the week in order to attend the academy, and returned home to New York on weekends.

It wasn't the kind of good news I'd hoped for. Losing her bracelet now seemed better in comparison. I'd hoped that Wendy would get settled into a rewarding career (working with children, not "stiffs") before she settled down with a husband and family. I wanted her to take time to sow her oats, and then have the confidence that she was making the right decision about sharing her life with someone. It was the most important decision she'd ever make, and I wanted it to be a wise one. I felt as if she were rushing headlong into this relationship. I tried to sound happy about the news, but I didn't know whether to be elated for Wendy or pray that, like all other things, "this too shall pass."

I opted to pray, but my prayers apparently fell on deaf ears. Or, perhaps my prayers were answered, but in a way I have yet to understand. A few months later, Wendy returned to the Midwest with her fiancé on her arm, the arm that once held her charm bracelet. I met the two of them at my front door the afternoon they arrived home to Kansas. Her fiancé looked straight at me with unwavering eyes as he held Wendy's arm in a possessive manner. His demeanor made me uncomfortable. It was as if he were daring me not to accept him as my future son-in-law. I wouldn't give him that satisfaction. I did my best to return the young man's stare.

"Mom, I'd like you to meet my fiancé, Clay Pitt."

Clay Pitt? Who would name their child Clay Pitt? Of course, not too many people can pull off any name that ends in "Pitt" unless their first name happens to be Brad. And technically, it was Clayton Oliver Pitt. Surely his parents realized other people would shorten his name to Clay, either out of convenience or spite.

But then, who am I to judge others on their name-picking abilities? A woman who named her own daughter Wendy, after a *Peter Pan* character, is now casting stones? Well, yes, but I had a very good excuse. After a long Tuesday, in excruciatingly painful labor, I finally delivered my daughter early on a Wednesday morning. I was exhausted and not feeling too creative when somebody wandered into the room with a birth certificate and asked me what I wanted to call the new baby girl. Call her a cab, I need a nap, I wanted to say. Chester was outside passing out cigars. Wendy sounded like Wednesday but was easier to spell, and made more sense than naming her February, so she was named Wendy Starr. I think any woman who's ever given birth can relate.

My thoughts soon drifted back to Clay. Or Clayton Oliver Pitt, I should say. His preppy monogrammed golf shirts would read COP. How fitting that he would grow up to be a police officer! I despised him on sight. His condescending voice grated on my nerves. He had a look about him that said: I'm the toughest, most self-possessed guy you'll ever meet, and don't you forget it.

Clay was a nice-looking man, however. I had to give credit where it was due. He was about six feet tall, brown-haired, green-eyed, and had a slim-hipped, broad-shouldered, muscular build. Clay was definitely easy on the eyes. But he was arrogant and overbearing, and had a chip on his shoulder the size of Ayers Rock. He wasn't at all the type of man I'd expect Wendy to find attractive.

My opinion of Clay didn't improve much, but I soon became adept at hiding my true feelings from Wendy. There was something about Clay that I didn't trust, but I couldn't quite put my finger on it in those early days. Even now, I have no concrete reason to distrust him, although suspected murder is a good start.

It was difficult for me to believe that Clay could kill his wife, a young woman who was expecting his child. In fact, it was hard for me to believe that any human being could be capable of this kind of atrocious behavior. For anybody to take another human's life was incomprehensible to me. Except possibly in the rare circumstance of self-defense, where a person's life was being threatened and killing an attacker was the only option.

But Clay was intolerant and quick-tempered. I'd observed him losing his cool over a very insignificant matter on a couple of occasions. I had once watched him snap at Wendy for not leaving steaks on the grill long enough, and then complain throughout the meal about the toughness of the meat. As Wendy would say, "He went ballistic."

Knowing what I know now, I think who'd know better than a cop, someone training as a homicide detective, no less, how to commit the perfect crime and get away with it?

THREE

This whole ordeal started at the small, local library where I volunteer as an assistant librarian two days a week. I was helping a young man research who'd won the men's Boston Marathon in 2001. The winner was Lee Bong-Ju, but that's beside the point.

We were searching through newspaper databases on microfilm because the small local library has not yet added Internet access to their program. (A wealthy citizen had pledged three complete computer systems, so the old-fashioned library would soon be reluctantly dragged, kicking and screaming, into the twenty-first century.)

The library also didn't keep the *Boston Globe* in their archives, so we chose to search through the April 2001 editions of the *New York Times,* hoping to find the news from the day after the marathon. Justin, the young man I was assisting, knew only that the race was held yearly in the month of April. He was considering the idea of writing a freelance article on the 2001 men's champion because Bong-Ju was the only competitor to win the annual event in thirteen years who wasn't from Kenya. Justin knew the man was from Korea, but couldn't recall his name. I can see where a name like Lee Bong-Ju wouldn't stick in your mind forever.

While the two of us were looking through microfilm clips, a headline leaped off the page at me: Clayton Pitt Under Cloud of Suspicion. It was a short article at the bottom of the fourth page. I nearly fell off the chair. Justin was eyeing me with concern, having noted my sudden odd behavior. I removed the film with jerky, spastic motions, and stammered, "Thought I recognized that name for a second, but I'm probably mistaken. I'll read it more thoroughly later."

My pathetic attempt at appearing nonchalant failed, but Justin had too many other things on his mind to dwell on my silliness for long. We quickly scanned through articles until we found the one we were searching for. I was never so happy to see someone's name as I was to see Lee Bong-Ju's. I'd lost interest in the runner from Korea and was itching to get back to the microfilm on the desk beside me.

After Justin had thanked me and strolled away, I reinserted the microfilm into the viewing machine with trembling fingers. I was so engrossed in this effort that an explosion could have leveled the building and left it in piles of rubble all around me, and I wouldn't have noticed. I shook my head as if I thought that would help clear it and give a chance for reality to set back in. I slowly read the article again.

Boston police academy standout, Clayton "Clay" Pitt, is being questioned due to the recent disappearance of his wife, Eliza Pitt, who was last seen in the parking lot of Schenectady's Food Pantry grocery store on Fourteenth Street early in the afternoon on April 12. Mr. Pitt has been unable to provide an adequate explanation to authorities regarding his whereabouts on that day. Chief investigator, Detective Ron Glick, stated Mr. Pitt has not officially been named as a suspect, but he is under a "cloud of suspicion" at this time. Pitt has been staying at a Boston motel during the week while attending the police academy. He spends weekends at his home in Schenectady, New York, where he and Eliza have resided since their 1996 marriage. The Pitts, both thirty, celebrated their fifth anniversary in March and are expecting their first child in July.

I had to read it again, and then one more time. I couldn't believe what I was seeing. Could this be a different Clay Pitt? Obviously there were a lot of clay pits, but how many human Clay Pitts could there be? How many Clayton "Clay" Pitts lived in New York, were thirty years old, and were enrolled in the police academy in Boston? Not many I presumed.

I was nearly bowled over by the thought that my new son-in-law was a potential killer, a sadistic murderer who could kill one spouse and replace her with another two years later. I sat back in my chair as questions zipped through my mind. Was Clay guilty or not? Was Wendy in mortal danger? Could another raw T-bone push her husband over the edge? What if Clay went really "ballistic"? Could a little marital spat escalate to the point of murder? I needed to find out the truth, one way or the other, or I'd never get another good night's sleep again.

I read the short article one last time, hopeful it was only a matter of needing stronger reading glasses. No such luck, I soon discovered. My vision had not deteriorated. The part about Clay staying at a Boston motel confused me a bit. I could've sworn that Wendy had told me he'd been staying with a friend there during the week. Perhaps he'd moved in with a friend following the disappearance of his wife.

I looked stealthily around the room and thrust the microfilm down into my pocket, as nervously as if shoplifting a diamond-studded watch. I knew there was a good possibility that I'd need to refer to the article again. I also snatched up films covering the following several weeks of the New York Times in case there were subsequent articles about the case. What were the chances anyone else would need to research those exact dates in the near future? Slim to none. I would return the films at a later date, when I no longer had a need for them.

What to do now? Wendy had to be warned that her husband could be a homicidal maniac, didn't she? Would warning her place my own life in peril? Worse yet, would it jeopardize my daughter's life? Would Wendy accept my news as a mother's attempt to protect her own flesh and blood, or would she view it as a mother's attempt to stick her nose in where it didn't belong? I didn't want to appear as if I were trying to come between Wendy and her new husband, as satisfying as that'd be. It would be no easy task to make Wendy see that the man she felt the sun rose and set on was not as flawless as she perceived him to be. I didn't want to take a chance of alienating my daughter in the process of trying to protect her. It seemed a no-win situation.

What to do? What to do? I rubbed my temples with the tips of my fingers as I considered my next move. I didn't think Wendy knew that Clay had been married before and that his wife had mysteriously disappeared. She wasn't the kind to have given him the time of day had she known he was a murder suspect.

Wendy was also not one to watch the news or read the paper, except on rare occasions. She found the news depressing, she'd told me on numerous occasions. But being oblivious to current events could have made Wendy vulnerable in this situation. Yes, I concluded, it was entirely possible that, living in Massachusetts, she'd have no knowledge of events happening in New York. Keeping up with the crimes taking place in New York could become a full-time job. The more I thought about it, the more I was certain that Wendy was completely unaware of Clay's past. The question was whether or not it was my responsibility to make her aware of it. Didn't Clay, himself, owe it to his new bride to fill her in on what most people would consider important events from his past? If he were truly innocent, would he hide the details from her? It didn't seem likely.

If I didn't warn my daughter and she became his next victim, could I live with that on my conscience? If my intervention caused a rift in their marriage, and Clay turned out to be completely innocent, could I live with that instead? But, I asked myself, wasn't it something I had to risk to make sure no harm came to my child?

I gave it serious thought on my way over to Wendy and Clay's new home in Kansas City, Kansas, just seven or eight blocks north of my own. I was hoping I'd come to the right decision on the way and that Clay would not be home when I arrived.

Unfortunately, Clay was home, talking in the front yard with his friends. He appeared more evil than ever to me, and even his friends had taken on a sinister look in his presence. I chickened out and fled home to hide in my own humble abode while I pondered the situation.

Sitting in my family room later, my feet propped up on the coffee table, a cup of espresso in my hand, I found myself almost wishing I'd never accidentally run across the newspaper article about the murder. But I believed nothing happened by accident, and there are no coincidences. I'd always felt things happen for a reason.

I was the one who'd been given the message, and I couldn't live with myself if I sat back and did nothing. I had to do whatever I could to protect my only child. I had to make a trip to Schenectady, New York. I helped people with research all the time in my volunteer work. Now it was time to do a little in-depth research and investigating for myself. It was time to find out what really happened to Eliza Pitt.

FOUR

I spent the next few days getting ready to make the trip to New York. It seemed like a good excuse to refresh my wardrobe, so a lot of my time was consumed at the local mall and at several of my favorite boutiques. I had my hair trimmed and drew cash out of the bank. I scoured through about a month's worth of the *New York Times* from April and May of 2001. I was disappointed to find only a few more short articles about the Eliza Pitt murder case.

"Battered Body Identified as Eliza Pitt" was the headline that really caught my eye. The article stated that dental records and DNA tests had positively proven the body to be that of Clayton Pitt's wife. Eliza's brutally abused body had been found two weeks after her disappearance by a hiker from nearby Schenectady. The hiker had stumbled across the remains of Clay's first wife in the Adirondack Mountains, north of Schenectady. There'd been little progress in determining who'd been responsible for her death. There'd been no irrefutable evidence linking her husband, Clayton, to the murder. As of yet, no polygraph test had been given or requested. Why were they giving him the benefit of the doubt? I wondered. Wasn't the victim's spouse always the primary suspect in a murder case like this one?

I hoped to get a lot more information from the local police department when I arrived in Schenectady. I even purchased a notebook to record all the details I uncovered about the case.

All that remained to do was to come up with a good excuse for my intended absence of undetermined length. I knew if Wendy were to try to contact me and be unsuccessful, she'd panic. I didn't want to scare her, but I obviously couldn't tell her I was going to Clay's hometown of Schenectady without raising a red flag. I'm sure Schenectady, New York, is a very nice town, but why would I go there on the spur of the moment, and then stay there for an extended amount of time? Off the top of my head, I couldn't think of one good falsehood that would be believable. I'm not a very accomplished liar as it is. Like Wendy, I could never look someone in the eye and tell a bald-faced lie. When attempting to deceive someone, we both become intently fascinated with our fingernails. And that happens even if we're only slightly stretching the truth. We both seem to stutter and, if it's a real whopper, we become afflicted with an involuntary reaction of popping our knuckles with an intensity that could crack walnuts in half. Wendy never could get away with anything as a child because I knew all the signs to look for. If I couldn't come up with an excuse that had at least some measure of truth in it, Wendy would know I was fibbing. She knew all the telltale signs too.

To force myself to think of something else for a while, I went up to my computer room to check my e-mail. I'd recently turned my third bedroom into an office when I realized I had too much space for company. It's not that a volunteer library assistant is in dire need of a home office; it's just that I have a few high-maintenance relatives who have a maximum appeal period of about three days. After three days I'm struggling to remember why I invited them to visit me in the first place. Three days of schlepping around, looking bored and hungry, rearranging my knickknacks, and leaving dirty towels on the bathroom floor is occasionally more than I can handle. And sometimes it's just nice to be able to highly recommend the

Comfort Inn up the street.

I logged on and was surprised to have only three unread messages. One of them offered me a lower interest rate on my home mortgage, a mortgage that's been paid off for almost two decades. The second was a diet promising a thirty-pound weight loss in three weeks or less. Not interested. I could accomplish that in about three seconds by firing up a chainsaw and lopping off a leg. Right now, while I'm relying heavily on comfort foods, lopping off a leg sounded less painful than giving up ice cream and potato chips. Hey, I had another one, didn't I?

The last e-mail was in response to a query I'd sent out earlier in the day. It was from Stone Van Patten, a representative of an online jewelry company called Pawley's Island Jewelers. In his message he assured me they carried very nice twenty-four-carat gold bracelets. Although I hadn't asked him to, he said he'd also be happy to help me try to replace Wendy's charms if I could send him a list and description of the lost ones. He said they may not be identical, but they'd be similar and every bit as nice. In closing, he stated it was very sweet of me to go to all the expense and trouble to replace my daughter's bracelet and charms. I must be a very special mother, he said.

"Very special mother?" Gee, I liked Stone already. I liked anybody who considered me special. I could use a little more "Stone" in my life right now. I'd been feeling a little neglected and out of sorts since Wendy and Clay's wedding. It was as if I'd suddenly realized that my baby had truly left the nest, and I was now on my own forever.

I tried to brush the sense of melancholy aside as I clicked on the "reply" icon. I thought it was very considerate of Mr. Van Patten to offer to assist me, and I told him so in my response. I hadn't figured out yet how to replace the charms without actually revisiting about two dozen cities scattered across the entire United States, not to mention Paris. I thanked him sincerely and included a description of all of the charms I could recall.

"Where is Pawley's Island?" I typed at the close of my reply. I didn't recall ever reading about that island in any of my travel literature.

When I checked my e-mail once more before going to bed that evening, I had another message from Mr. Van Patten—Stone, I should say. "Call me Stone, please," he'd requested in his last message.

Stone wrote that replacing most of the charms, if not all, would take a few weeks but shouldn't present any big problems. He'd enjoy working on the assignment as a break from his normal routine. He ended with, "Pawley's Island is just south of Myrtle Beach, South Carolina, in the Grand Strand area. It's not the typical island you might visualize. Have you ever had the opportunity to visit here before? I noticed that your daughter had no charms from South Carolina."

Before signing off I sent another message of appreciation and a negative reply to his question. Although I knew it to be a beautiful state, I'd never visited Myrtle Beach or Pawley's Island or any other part of South Carolina. But someday I would make it there, I promised.

I spent a restless night tossing and turning, counting sheep until I was sick of them. After I crawled out of bed in the morning, I took a long, hot shower and then took even longer reading through the morning paper. I drank nearly a full pot of coffee and forced myself to pour what little remained in the carafe down the sink only when I was tempted to do cartwheels down the hallway. I was keyed up, but still procrastinating on my phone call to Wendy. I'd yet to come up with a reason to leave town that I thought she'd believe. I found myself reading a less than titillating article about future renovation plans for the building that housed the local chapter of the boilermakers union. I decided I was carrying procrastination a bit too far.

As a more interesting stall tactic, I laid down the paper and went upstairs to check my e-mail. One message told me I was pre-approved for a platinum MasterCard and another involved spy cams and farm animals. I immediately deleted both and read the other message from Stone, the jeweler.

"I'll get right to work on locating the replacement charms and will let you know from time to time how I'm coming along on the project. Someday, when you arrive in South Carolina, call me and I'll be happy to be your tour guide. Take care, Stone."

His phone number was included at the end of his note. I started to delete the message but then had a twinge of guilt. For some neurotic reason, I felt as if he could see me through the computer screen and was waiting for me to record his number. I jotted his name and number down on a post-it note and stuck it to the side of my monitor. I'd ignore it for a week or so, and then discard it without remorse.

"Thank you, Stone. Someday I might just take you up on your tour guide offer. You take care too. Sincerely, Lexie," I typed, and then clicked on "Send."

Yeah, of course I would. And some other day, while hell was freezing over, I might just bungee jump off the Kaw River Bridge. Anything was possible, wasn't it? Stone certainly seemed like a decent, pleasant individual, but I wasn't looking for complications right now. I had enough on my plate as it was.

Yes, anything was indeed possible, I told myself again. And then it hit me. I now had a viable excuse for leaving town. Wendy wouldn't like it, I was certain, but it was the best I could come up with at the moment. My excuse would have at least a grain of truth to it, if but a very tiny grain. I'd met a man on the Internet and was going on a trip East to get to know him better. Well, I had met Stone on the Internet. And I'm sure that in the course of communicating with him about the charms, I'd get to know him a little better. The fact that I didn't plan to be within five hundred miles of the fellow was just a minor detail.

FIVE

"Mom, I'm sorry, but I can't talk right now. I have a pan of biscuits that needs to come out of the oven. Can I just run by your place later?"

No, that wouldn't do, I thought. I doubted I could fabricate as well in my own home. I'd feel more confident on foreign ground. Okay, less trapped on foreign ground. I really did dread a face-to-face confrontation with Wendy. I could leave her house whenever I wanted to, but could hardly shove her out my own front door when I wanted to end the conversation. I'd have to use at least a little tact and decorum, two admirable traits that did not come naturally to me.

"How about if I just stop by your house in about an hour?" I asked her. "I have to go to Wal-Mart anyway. I'm going out of town, and I need a few last minute items." You know, I said to myself, a magnifying glass, DNA test strips, fingerprint kit, and other must-have travel items.

"Where are you going?" Wendy asked.

"I'll explain when I get there. Don't let those biscuits burn," I cautioned, and quickly replaced the handset.

Oh boy, here goes. Suddenly the urge to pop my knuckles was intense.

Wendy looked tired. Her long auburn hair looked stringy and unkempt. She was a few inches taller than I, standing at about five feet, five inches or so, and she'd always been extremely thin.

31

She's one of those women other women despise solely because of their metabolism—the type you expect to whine that they have problem keeping weight on their frames. The type who'd say, "I can eat eighteen thousand calories a day and not gain an ounce," while licking chocolate frosting off their fingers.

Actually, Wendy has never been one to boast about her ability to eat like a rhinoceros and stay stick slim. She doesn't even nag me about my weight when I start building on layers of insulation every winter. That's just one of the things I love so much about her.

To be honest, however, as envious as I was of her metabolism, I was sure Wendy would look more attractive with about ten extra pounds. When she's worn down, she looks haggard, and the gauntness in her face is even more pronounced, as it had been recently. She looked like she'd been under a lot of pressure, and I felt bad that I was about to add to her worries.

"Hi, Mom. Come in and have a seat in the kitchen. I've just made a fresh pot of coffee. You look like you could use a cup."

She must not have seen me doing cartwheels down her driveway. "Yes, dear, a cup of coffee would be wonderful," I said.

"So, tell me, where are you going?"

"Myrtle Beach, South Carolina."

"Whatever for?" she asked, sipping her coffee.

"T-to—to meet a man."

"What? What did you say?" There was disbelief is her voice, as she spewed coffee across the kitchen table.

As Wendy eyed me suspiciously, I popped several of my knuckles before I continued. "I'm meeting a very nice gentleman who lives there."

"Whatever for?" Wendy asked again.

Couldn't you make it easy for me, dear, and just nod your head in acceptance? I'm doing all this for you—to protect you.

So please don't drag me through the coals over annoying little details, I said under my breath. My knuckles were already beginning to swell.

I checked each of my cuticles and began to ramble. "Well, dear, as you know, I've been widowed for almost twenty years. I never felt you'd accept another man in my life, either as a substitute father figure to you, or as an object of affection to me. And I didn't particularly want to throw myself back into the dating scene anyway. But now that you're grown up and married, I've met a man I'm interested in and would like to get to know better. I can almost guarantee it won't go any further than friendship, but I want to give it a chance so I won't regret it later. I'm not getting any younger, you know. And it's kind of lonely for me these days."

I stopped to catch my breath, and to get an emery board out of my purse to smooth out a jagged fingernail I'd just noticed.

Wendy's mouth was hanging open in shock and dismay. I could read the thoughts flashing through her mind as if she'd spoken them out loud. My mother has taken leave of her senses. Dementia has set in. And she's lying about something. That much is obvious. Wendy turned her chair to face me and attempted to look me in the eye. I was too preoccupied with that jagged nail.

"What's his name?" Wendy asked.

"St-st-tone Van Patten." Here we go, interrogation time. Wasn't this intense questioning routine once part of my job description as her mother?

"Stone? Did you say Stone? What kind of name is Stone?"

Very much like Clay, if you really think about it, I wanted to say. What did it really matter what the man's name was?

"He's a jeweler, honey, a highly respected jeweler, so I'm sure that Stone is just a nickname. His real name is probably something too common like Bill or Bob," I said defensively.

"Where'd you meet him?"

"On the Internet."

She slammed her hand down with a vivid expletive. I jumped back in my chair in surprise. "You've got to be kidding," she shouted. "Are you totally nuts, Mom?"

"No, I, er, he just—"

"Mom, this world is full of weirdoes, whackos, and perverts. Are you aware of that? How old is he?" Wendy spat out "he" like it was another word for pond scum.

I only knew Stone to be somewhere between puberty and social security, so I opted for a generic answer. "Oh, you know, a b-b-baby-boomer like myself."

I gulped down half my coffee in one swallow and it burnt my throat badly. I choked, I gagged, and after a prolonged coughing fit, I stood up to leave. "Listen, Wendy, I'd love to stay and chat, but I really have a lot of things I need to get done. I'm sure that once you get used to the idea you'll be okay with it."

Wendy snorted. She actually snorted in derision. "I doubt it, Mom," she said. "And we're not through with this discussion by any means."

I was afraid of that. I loved my daughter more than life itself, but she was sorely trying my patience.

Wendy continued, "And I expect you to stop by here to talk to me again before you leave town. I want to know more about this Rock guy!"

"It's Stone."

"Rock, Stone, whatever . . ."

I walked out her front door with my chin resting against my chest, lower lip protruding and quivering slightly. Exactly when had our roles become reversed? I wondered. I felt like I'd just been chastised and sent to my room, my punishment to be meted out at a later time. Oh well, at least I'd been granted a small reprieve.

Early Thursday morning I stopped by the dental clinic to have my teeth cleaned and x-rayed. The dental hygienist used a new tool that employed a powerful and painful jet of cold water to sandblast the plaque off my teeth. It was like a Waterpik on steroids. I lay back in the chair, grasping, like a lifeline, the tube that was suctioning gallons of water, blood, and saliva from the back of my throat. I was counting the ceiling tiles in an attempt not to scream in agony and bolt from the room. It was then I remembered why I subjected myself to this modern form of water torture only every few years instead of biannually, as recommended. I felt immense relief when the cleaning was completed even though my gums were throbbing, and, no doubt, red and puffy.

I nodded absentmindedly as the hygienist chided me on my poor flossing habits and warned me of my potential for gingivitis, due to the deep pockets between my teeth and gums. My mind was already on the other tasks I needed to accomplish before the day was over. It wasn't like I hadn't heard it all before anyway.

After leaving the dental clinic, I took my Jeep Wrangler to the Dodge dealer to have it serviced. It'd been running a little rough and was due for an oil change anyway. Kenny, the service manager, promised to give it a thorough checkup. He'd change the oil and check the tires, brakes, fluid levels, spark plugs, filters, and belts. He thought the carburetor sounded as if it was running a little rich and that the air filter was probably clogged. The Jeep was only two years old and still had less than 15,000 miles on it, so Kenny didn't anticipate any major repairs. It was a slow day at the garage, and he assured me he'd have it ready to pick up in a couple of hours.

During the long drive to New York from Kansas, I didn't want to experience any car trouble. Breaking down on the interstate is a terrifying ordeal these days. Whenever my vehicle breaks down, and somebody stops to assist me, I immediately question his motives. Why would he want to help me? Is he really a molester, a carjacker, a drug addict, or some other kind of dangerous thug? As I stand on the shoulder, hood up on my car, looking helplessly down at a motor that is refusing to cooperate, I sense that motorists are speeding by looking at me, wondering what kind of thug I am too. It's a scary situation for both sides. I raise the hood and stare at the motor only to make it obvious that the car has broken down, not because I can tell the difference between a manifold and a shoebox.

So far this Jeep has never stranded me. It's the perfect low profile, inconspicuous vehicle for a Sherlock Holmes wannabe to go amateur sleuthing in—canary yellow, with lots of chrome and lights. I've always been big on accessories, so the Jeep is equipped with a roof rack, running boards, taillight covers, chrome grip handles, brush guard with lights, roll bar with lights, and of course, a spare tire cover with a painting of Tweety Bird bending over and mooning the vehicle behind me. To complete the package, it sports off-road tires the size of those you'd see on an earthmover or a Caterpillar D9. This vehicle had never been off the pavement, nor did I expect it ever would be, but a Jeep cries out for oversized tires just so it won't look wimpy like a Ford Taurus or a Mercury Sable.

I sat down in the waiting room and sifted through fourteen issues of *Car and Driver* while I drank three cups of vending machine coffee that looked thicker than the motor oil Kenny was draining out of my Jeep. I glanced at my watch and noticed that exactly seven minutes had passed since I turned the keys over to the mechanic.

I walked to the pay phone and called Wendy to come pick me

up. She wasn't scheduled to begin her new job at the county coroner's office for two more weeks. I decided to bite the bullet and get round two of the inquisition over.

Wendy was in high spirits when she picked me up. As we headed back toward her neighborhood, she told me Clay had been offered a detective position with the KCK Homicide Division. It was the position he'd most wanted to land when he'd distributed his resume and applications, Wendy declared, with a great deal of pride evident in her voice.

"He's so glad he's going to work with the Kansas City Kansas Police Department," Wendy said. She seemed unusually excited and bubbly. "Clay said that there are a lot more murders in Kansas City than in Shawnee, Lenexa, or any of these smaller, suburban, metropolitan areas."

"Yes," I agreed. "Lots of murders—I'm sure that's a wonderful thing. Nothing like job security, right? I know Clay must be thrilled."

I wanted to tell Wendy that her new husband was a menace to society. If it took one to know one, he'd probably be an expert at weeding out killers. "Oh, yes, Mom," Wendy said. "We both are. He starts this Monday. I'll have over a week to myself—during the days at least—before I start my job."

"That will be nice, I'm sure," I said, sincerely.

"So, Mom, you're still determined to go through with this, huh?"

"Yes, honey, I am."

"You're going to drive twelve hundred miles to go see some man you only know from chatting with him over the Internet, and you don't think that's a bit insane, and maybe just a touch impulsive and dangerous? Mom, you don't know this guy from Adam!"

Gosh, I don't even know Adam. I wasn't going to drive twelve hundred miles to see Stone. I said I was going to get to know him better, not "see" him. I am not a liar. I am not a liar, I repeated over and over to myself. "Wendy, that's just part of the reason I'm going back East. I've always heard the fall colors back in that area are fantastic, and I thought while I was back there enjoying the sights, I might as well meet Stone somewhere for dinner and a drink. That's all I have in mind. I'll be staying in a little bed and breakfast by myself, not at his place. There is absolutely nothing for you to worry about. I'll be f-f-fine."

I looked over at Wendy as she drove, rather erratically, down Seventy-Fifth Street. She looked unconvinced. "R-r-really," I added lamely.

Suddenly the thought of being tortured by the dental hygienist again seemed preferable to conversing with my own child. My gums throbbed in an involuntary reaction to the recollection of my hour from hell at the dental clinic.

I changed the subject then and began talking about a three-day sale at the JCPenney outlet. The ploy worked. We even stopped at the outlet, and I picked up a Minolta Maxxum camera outfit that had been marked down thirty percent. My old camera had become unreliable, and I'd have to take pictures of the fall colors back East, if nothing else. I, of course, would have to return to Kansas with an album full of tree photos to validate my newly revised story.

We entered Wendy's house through the garage, loaded down with several sacks full of household items she'd purchased for her new home. It was the first time I'd been in their basement rec room since Wendy and Clay had moved in. The furniture was grouped in front of a wood-burning stove. Against the far wall was a TV with a screen the size of a garage door, and there was a bull moose head hanging over a brown leather couch.

"Wow, that was quick!" I said.

"Huh?"

"Your taxidermist's motto should be 'You bang 'em, we'll

hang 'em—fast!"

Wendy looked flustered for a second, and then it dawned on her I was talking about the moose head. "That's a different mount, Mom. Clay brought this one from New York. He bagged it somewhere back East."

"Oh, I see." I didn't really have a clue why anyone would want one dead moose head in his home, much less two. The next couple of hours were enjoyable. Clay was out somewhere with his weight-lifting buddies, probably drinking beer and smashing the cans against his forehead. Wendy and I visited, laughed, and drank espresso until Kenny called Wendy's number to let me know my Jeep was ready to pick up.

Wendy was still upset with me, but she'd resigned herself to the fact I was going to South Carolina to meet the psychotic pervert with the ridiculous name, and nothing she said or did was going to stop me. For the moment, that was good enough for me.

Six

The sun was just peeking up over the horizon as I approached the Columbus, Ohio, city limits. I'd spent the first night of the trip in a little budget motel near Indianapolis. It had offered reasonable rates, and had a nearby diner and gas station. More importantly, I didn't see any bugs in my room large enough to cart off my suitcase.

I'd awoken early, too excited to sleep, so I'd taken off again before sunrise. I filled up with gas at the all-night station down the street, and purchased an Indiana Hoosiers travel mug full of hot, but tasteless, coffee.

By the time the first signs of dawn appeared in the eastern sky—pink and purple streaks across the lower part of the horizon, fading to light blue higher up—I was beginning to get hungry and restless. I was still reeling from having struck and killed a raccoon that had darted out onto the road in front of me. I'd pulled over to check on its condition, hoping it wasn't beyond saving, but I was saddened to discover that it had died instantly upon impact. I scooted its lifeless body off the pavement into the grassy area beyond the shoulder and said a quick prayer on the raccoon's behalf.

Driving along, keeping an eye out for a café, I thought about Wendy's reaction to my announcement that I was traveling to the east coast to meet a man I'd encountered over the Internet. It seemed to me that she was as concerned about my safety as she was about the fact I was considering a romantic interlude with a man. I don't think it was the fact that I was meeting a man so much as the manner in which I was going about it.

Thinking back several years, I recalled the time Wendy had tried to set me up on a blind date with the divorced father of one of her friends. So at least she wasn't completely opposed to the idea of me dating. Perhaps she'd even realized that I wanted a man in my life before I'd come to that conclusion myself. I was still not convinced that was the case, but I admitted to myself I was beginning to feel a twinge of loneliness and depression since Wendy's wedding a month and a half earlier. Wendy had Clay to share her life with now. Who did I have to discuss the mundane aspects of my day with at the dinner table each evening? I could hardly call Wendy umpteen times a day, now that she was married. I could adopt a cute little orange tabby I'd seen at the animal shelter, but I wasn't certain that was the answer either. A cat's vocabulary was pretty much limited to "feed me," "pet me," and "get out of my way." I needed a little more stimulating conversation and companionship than a kitten had to offer.

I was almost shocked by the direction my thoughts had taken. It had been a long time since I'd given a man a second thought, or even a second glance. I was very accustomed to my independence, and reasonably comfortable with my current lifestyle. I wasn't sure I could adapt to such a big change at this stage in my life. Still a gentleman—a thoughtful, caring, and mature individual—might be fun to spend a little time with, now and then. Oh, good grief, what was I thinking? I needed stronger coffee; that much was obvious. And maybe a little fresh air, I thought as I cracked open the window.

I shook my head to revert my wandering attention back to driving. No sense endangering the wildlife population and leaving a trail of roadkill in my wake.

As I continued east on I-70, I admired the pastoral scenes on either side of the road. There were three horses running through a field of newly baled hay on my left, a young boy and an elderly man walking toward a small farm pond on my right. The two were wearing matching bib overalls and carrying fishing poles over their shoulders. They appeared as if they could be discussing the trophy fish they were hoping to catch.

I took a sip of coffee and cranked the volume up on the stereo. One of my favorite Merle Haggard tunes drifted out of the speakers, and I sang along with the confidence of someone who knew she couldn't carry a tune in a dump truck—much less a basket—and didn't really care.

"Big city turn me loose and set me free," I sang off-key as I beat my fingers on the steering wheel in reasonable beat with the music. I felt completely in tune with the words of the song, emotionally, if not audibly. I loved the country, its scents and scenes, and its laid-back atmosphere. But I also loved the conveniences of city life, even though I felt the crowded confines were unbearably stifling, and sometimes frightening. I had experienced both worlds and found both had good points and bad. The Kansas suburb I now lived in offered a comfortable mixture of both, and that greatly appealed to me.

I'd felt a great sense of apprehension and uneasiness leaving Shawnee to go to Schenectady, not knowing what I might discover about my new son-in-law. I noticed that the farther east I drove, the more nervous and uptight I felt.

Up ahead a flashing sign stretched across the front of a barn-shaped building. Redwood Café, it read, and according to the sign it was home to the best breakfast buffet in town. Although I normally ate a light breakfast, or no breakfast at all, this morning a plate piled high with cholesterol-laden bacon and eggs sounded like just the balm I needed to calm my nerves. If nothing else, I reasoned that it was better to be anxious on a full stomach than an empty one. I steered the Jeep down the next exit ramp and turned left toward the café.

As it turned out, the fall colors back east were even better than I'd anticipated, and I found myself taking photo after photo. Each bend in the road brought a picture-postcard scene more incredible than the last. I was particularly proud of a shot I'd taken earlier in the trip of large tobacco leaves drying as they hung from the rafters of an open-ended barn. The sun shining through the barn should make it a fascinating photo. I hoped the new Minolta produced the type of photographs promised in the company's advertisements.

I'd booked a room at a bed and breakfast right in downtown Schenectady. It was on Union Street, across from a cozy-looking diner where I figured I could eat many of my meals. The white-haired proprietor at the Camelot B&B was a feisty, little old lady named Harriet Sparks. She looked to be about a hundred years old, but ran around the place like she was eight. Where did she get that kind of energy? I wondered in awe.

Harriet chain-smoked unfiltered Pall Malls down to the point the calluses on her fingers were glowing red. She weighed about one hundred pounds, and before I could stop her, she had hoisted my ninety-five-pound suitcase up the steep staircase to my room. She sprinted up the steps and then waited for me to catch up at the top of the staircase. I followed her to a room at the far end of the wide hallway.

"Ya need anything, sweetie, ya just holler. Ya hear?" Harriet's raspy voice made me think of a western Kansas pheasant. It sounded like she had a load of gravel in her craw. "I know most everything 'bout everybody in these here parts."

I nodded and knew instantly that Harriet would become a friend, and hopefully, a valuable source of information. I thought of Justin's Korean marathoner as I said, "Say, listen, Harriet, I'm thinking about doing a freelance article on a murder that took place here in Schenectady a couple of years ago. Would you know anything about the Eliza Pitt case, by any chance?"

"As much as anybody, I reckon. But the killing didn't take place here in Schenectady, sweetie. No sir-ee! He kilt that little gal up in dem mountains."

"Oh? Have they determined who murdered her then?"

"Well, not 'fficially, but it's as plain as my face that it were her old man that whacked her," Harriet said. "Don't take no rocket scientist to figure that one out."

Whacked? Harriet had been watching too many *NYPD Blue* shows. She sounded like Andy Sipowicz. "After I get settled, would you mind telling me what you know about the case? Tomorrow sometime, maybe?"

"Shore sweetie, any time. Like I said, I know most everything 'bout everybody in these here parts." With that, Harriet scurried off down the hallway, as if there were snakes that needed whacking in the basement.

I relaxed over dinner at the Union Street Diner across the street. The small cafe was dimly lit with only a handful of customers, but the food was excellent. I chose to eat sensibly and ordered one trip to the salad bar. I then piled about ten thousand calories' worth of macaroni salad, fruit salad, banana pudding, fresh bread, and other goodies on a platter that looked like something a pizza parlor might use for baking their jumbo supremes.

When I returned to the room, I unpacked my bag and set up my laptop computer on a little corner hutch. I planned to make occasional contact with Wendy, via e-mail, to rave about the vivid color of the trees and to let her know I was enjoying myself and doing fine. I hesitated to call her. I knew she had caller ID, and I hadn't thought to purchase a cell phone. A call from

Clay's hometown area code would not be a wise move on my part.

My small, but well-appointed, room was adorable. There was a four-poster bed with a canopy against the back wall, and a blue, white, and yellow spread that featured bright sunflowers. Belgian lace valances hung on both windows, and the antique dresser had a large oval mirror with scented candles on either side. A note under one of them read, "Feel free to burn me."

An old-fashioned rocking chair and the corner desk completed the furnishings. The entire house boasted nine-foot ceilings and hardwood floors. There were no less than a dozen different-colored throw rugs scattered about my small room. I could walk around the room all day long and never have my feet actually touch the floor. It was like wall-to-wall carpet in three-by-five-foot sections.

The bathroom assigned to my room was not connected, but it was behind the next door down the hallway. It had fuchsia-colored wallpaper and a huge turquoise and yellow bath mat. I was beginning to see that Harriet preferred her surroundings to be bright and bold. Her taste matched her colorful personality perfectly. It was nothing like the way I'd chosen to decorate my own home, but for some reason, I loved it and was charmed by Harriet's eccentric style. Perhaps it was because it was in such sharp contrast to my own home that it appealed to me.

I was relieved to feel very comfortable with the accommodations I'd booked over the Internet. As I undressed in the bathroom, I thought about how fortunate I was to have found this quaint little inn. It was ideal for me. I spent an hour lounging in a warm bath, nearly falling asleep in the deep, claw-footed tub. I then sent a quick e-mail to Wendy, stating only that I'd arrived safely at my destination and it had been an uneventful trip. I'd been on the road most of the day and I was exhausted. I logged off the computer, crawled into bed, and counted about two and a half sheep before drifting off into a much-needed slumber.

I woke up feeling refreshed the following morning, but still I didn't feel quite ready to begin delving into the mysterious disappearance and death of Clay's former wife. My procrastination tendencies were kicking in full force.

When I'd registered the previous day, Harriet hadn't mentioned the "breakfast" half of her B&B services. It was only 7:45, but I thought maybe I could catch her up and about and talk her out of a cup of coffee. I needed a fix for my caffeine addiction before I did anything else.

As I walked down the stairs, I heard lively music coming from the kitchen and recognized the tune as "Brick House" by The Commodores. I walked toward the sound of the music and found Harriet dancing and cleaning out the bottom of a large birdcage at the same time. It was an amusing and endearing sight.

"Morning," came a high-pitched greeting that was barely discernable over the loud music. "Morning, sweetie," the voice repeated. I looked up and saw the red tail of an African gray parrot as it flitted behind a large kettle atop the refrigerator.

Harriet flicked off the radio and turned toward me. "Morning, sleepyhead. Say hello to Sinbad." She gestured toward the parrot.

"Good morning, Harriet," I said. "Good morning, Sinbad. You sure are a pretty thing."

"Ah, horseshit," Sinbad responded as he paced back and forth across the appliance. "Horseshit, horseshit. Shut up, nasty thing. Sinbad's a bad boy, a bad boy. Damn bird."

Harriet snapped her towel at the foul-mouthed parrot and muttered, "Damn nasty-mouthed bird." It was easy to see from whom Sinbad had learned his colorful vocabulary.

"Did you sleep well, sweetie?" Harriet asked me. She gave me a cup from the cup rack and pointed toward a percolator on the stove.

"Oh yes, I slept like a log," I said. "Just need a shot of coffee to wake me up." I poured what appeared to be half coffee and half coffee grounds into a coffee cup labeled "Lady Luck Casino." I could easily picture Harriet slamming quarters into a slot machine and cussing like Sinbad when it didn't pay out.

I took a swallow of coffee and almost spat it out across the kitchen floor. I was wide awake instantly. This coffee even made the espresso I normally drank seem weak and vapid. After a few sips of Harriet's stout coffee, I'd be bouncing off the walls. It had to have been brewing for a long time. Harriet must have gotten up hours ago, I decided.

"Good, that's good. I was just thinking I otter go up and put a mirror under yer nose to see if you's still breathing," Harriet said. "Breakfast is served at six 'round here. I made your breakfast fer ya but tossed it out after a spell when ya didn't show up."

"Oh, Harriet, I'm so sorry. I didn't realize . . ."

Did Harriet forget she hadn't told me about breakfast, or did she just assume that everyone got up at the crack of dawn for a six o'clock feeding? With a sweep of her hand, Harriet waved off my apology. "S'okay, I knew ya had a long day yesterday, so I let ya be lazy and sleep in late. But after this, be down here at six fer breakfast. Ya hear?"

Oh my! I had gone and enlisted in boot camp! I'd have to set my alarm for five-thirty to be dressed and down in the kitchen by six. I didn't get up at five-thirty even if Ed McMahon and the prize patrol were at my front door, and much less for breakfast.

"Horseshit," Sinbad squawked. He'd taken the words right out of my mouth.

"Sure, Harriet. No problem," I said. I couldn't hurt this nice lady's feelings. She'd already wasted one breakfast on me. I told myself that tomorrow I'd have my lazy butt down at the kitchen table at six sharp.

"Sit down, girl," Harriet commanded. "I'll have yer plate ready in a jiff. Ya like poached eggs on toast, don't ya?"

I could barely stomach poached eggs. I liked eggs cooked over hard or not at all. But Harriet had already scrapped one meal because of me. I didn't feel like I could be choosy at that point, and I had no desire to look like a prima donna in her eyes. I felt I could tolerate runny eggs for one meal. If I could get Harriet's coffee down, I could suffer through anything. "Love them, Harriet. Thanks."

"Just be a sec."

"No hurry. Has everyone else eaten?"

"There ain't no one else, sweetie. This time of year is usually perty slow. You be my only lodger right now."

"Oh, I see. Well I love it here, and I'm so thankful I found your place on the Internet." It was the truth, although I was beginning to have second thoughts.

"Yeah, me too. Like I say befer, business been perty slow. My son set that 'puter deal up. Me, I don't do 'puters. Figure you can't teach an old dog new tricks," Harriet said, as she set a plate down in front of me. There was enough toast and runny eggs on the plate to feed a lumberjack, and I wasn't sure I could even get half of it down. "Chow down, sweetie. Time's a'wasting."

I reluctantly shoveled spoonfuls of half-raw eggs mixed with soggy toast into my mouth, knowing I was going to have to eat it all or be severely scolded for wasting perfectly good food. At least I would save money on meals while I was here. I wouldn't be hungry again until suppertime. If I ate like this all the time, I'd have to make room in my closet for an extra-large wardrobe.

I noticed that Harriet was watching me intently, apparently waiting for my evaluation of her cooking.

"This is wonderful, Harriet. Thanks."

"Ya like it, huh?"

"Yes, I sure do."

"Ya like it a lot?" Harriet asked, for more clarification.

"Oh yes, it's delicious." Please, Lord, don't let me upchuck on Harriet's table.

"Good, that's good. Ya want some peaches with that? They needs to be ate befer they go bad," Harriet offered.

Befer they go bad? As good as that sounds, no thanks. No way, Jose. That's where I draw the line. Poached eggs are one thing, but nothing on the verge of "going bad" is going to cross these lips.

"Oh, no Harriet, I couldn't," I said. "There's more on my plate now than I can handle. It's wonderful, but I've got to watch my weight, you know."

She eyed my thighs for a second and replied, "Yes, I guess yer right." Oh my, that one hurt. Harriet shook her head as if she'd just spied a woman at her kitchen table the size of a beached whale. I decided at that very moment that those pesky ten extra pounds would have to be dealt with in the near future. I started to push my half-finished plate away and grimaced as Harriet continued, "Oh well, them eggs won't hurt ya none, so after ya clean yer plate, we'll sit out on the porch with our coffee, and I'll tell ya what I know 'bout that little gal that got whacked by her old man."

There was a covered porch off the kitchen in the rear of the little inn that overlooked the most chaotic flower garden I'd ever seen. There were at least a hundred different kinds of flowers growing and scattered haphazardly about the backyard. It looked as if the entire area had been tilled and a hundred bags of mixed seeds broadcast from a hovering helicopter. There was a riot of color, but somehow it all resulted in a very soothing effect.

Looking closely, I saw a single tomato plant in the back corner, one bell pepper plant near the steps leading down from the porch, and in the very middle of the backyard was a solitary pumpkin. It was by far the largest pumpkin I'd ever seen in my entire forty-eight years. Harriet must have gone through a full gallon of Miracle-Gro on that one plant alone.

"Big critter, ain't it?" Harriet commented when she saw me staring at the humongous pumpkin.

"I'll say," I agreed. "If it had an antenna and a bud vase it could easily be mistaken for an orange VW bug. You need to enter that monster in the county fair, Harriet."

"Reckon I otter. Won't be worth a tinker's damn to eat—that size and all. But I ain't got the heart to whack it outta there. Maybe I'll make a jack-o'-lantern outta it and put it on the front porch come Hallerween. Fer the kiddies, ya know."

"Oh, yes, you should, Harriet. If I'm still here, I'll help you carve it."

Harriet had pointed me to a hanging hammock-type chair swinging from the rafters of the porch. Nestled in the seat was a green and white striped cushion. Harriet sat down opposite the chair on an upside-down five-gallon bucket that looked like it had been around as long as she had. There were spots where rust had eaten completely through the metal.

"Harriet, let me sit there. You take the chair. You've been working this morning, and I haven't," I said. I didn't want to imply I was offering the chair to her because she was old. Despite her age, I was certain that Harriet could work circles around me.

"Nah, rather sit here. Been sitting on this here bucket for years. Iffing I was to git too comfy, I'd git lazy."

I plopped myself down into the chair and sighed. It was like sitting on a cloud. I'd never sat in anything so comfortable in my entire life, and I could visualize myself spending all my free time here in this very spot.

I opened my notebook. Pen in hand, I felt I resembled the freelance writer that I was pretending to be.

"So, tell me, Harriet, what do you know about the Pitt case?"

"Well, ever body around here knows that the Pitt boy weren't no good. That much is fer shore. He'd been running 'round on Eliza fer a long time, iffing ya ask me. Clay's what they call a 'rounder' in these here parts. Likes to drink, fight, and pick up trashy broads. Ain't seen him 'round in a spell, but he used to chase tail down at that strip joint down the road, drunker than a skunk ever night. One night he got tanked up and shot the weathervane off the top of the sheriff's house. Spent the weekend in the slammer too, he did. Yes sir-ee! Shoulda left him there and thrown away the key."

"Wow, he sounds like a real pillar of sobriety, er, society," I said.

Harriet ignored, or didn't understand, my pun, and kept talking. "He's meaner than a snake too. Thumped his missus ever chance he got. Poor girl come awandering into Mabel's hair store one day with a cracked tooth and a split lip. Said a softball smacked her, but even that tongue-wagging, gossip hound, Mabel, knew that were a lie. Softball, hell, covering fer that no 'count husband of hers was what she were doing."

"Did Clay know that Eliza was expecting their child?"

"Shore he did. That's what set him off, iffing ya ask me. Didn't want to be shackled to the wife, much less no kid. That's why he did her in fer good, iffing ya ask me. It weren't no surprise to no one, I can tell ya that fer shore. Don't know why them damn silly cops ain't smart enough to see that. Says they ain't got no evidence. Why, bloody hell, that split lip otter had

51

been evidence enuff."

By this point I knew all I was going to get out of Harriet was her somewhat biased and speculative opinion. It sounded more like rumor and supposition than a factual accounting. Harriet hadn't told me one certifiable detail I could record in my notebook yet, but she was looking at me quizzically, so I jotted down, "abusive, drunk, adulterer, fighter, kid-hater." If nothing else, it seemed apparent that my son-in-law was not very well respected in "these here parts."

I told Harriet that was all I needed to know at that point, but I would no doubt be picking her brain more in the future. She seemed content with that. The hammock chair was so comfortable and I felt I needed to get my bearings before I dove into a full-fledged investigation, so I decided to take it easy the rest of the day and run over to the police department tomorrow. I'd brought along the latest best seller and wanted to sit on the porch, procrastinate, and read. I didn't want to think about what my son-in-law might do to my daughter. It was only about sixty degrees out, but by the time Harriet had finished talking, I had beads of sweat above my eyebrows.

I swiped the sleeve of my KU Jayhawks sweatshirt across my forehead and leaned back to relax in this small slice of heaven I'd just discovered, while Harriet rushed down to the yard to deadhead flagging blossoms off a patch of petunias.

SEVEN

The alarm clock went off at five-thirty the next morning and nearly scared ten years off my life. I was tempted to roll over and go back to sleep, but I could hear music downstairs and knew Harriet was in the kitchen cooking breakfast for me. I didn't want to disappoint her again, so I groaned and stretched, and grudgingly got up to get dressed. I wasn't accustomed to eating early and really just wanted coffee. I hoped Harriet was preparing a light meal, now that she knew I was watching my weight. Not peaches, or anything else about to turn green and furry, but a toasted bagel or a bowl of oatmeal wouldn't be too bad, even at the ungodly hour of six in the morning.

"Good morning, sweetie," Sinbad and Harriet said in unison as I entered the kitchen at a minute before six.

"Good morning," I said.

"Ya be right on time. Yer breakfast be ready in just a sec."

"Damn nuisance," Sinbad squawked.

I laughed at the parrot and removed a coffee cup from the cup rack. People are indeed creatures of habit, so I instinctively selected the "Lady Luck Casino" cup. I poured myself a cup of thick, chewy coffee and sat down at the table. Bad coffee was better than no coffee at all. After the first few swallows it was a little easier to get down.

I sipped my coffee cautiously while I watched Harriet dip a spatula into the skillet in front of her. It was clear that oatmeal and bagels were not on the breakfast menu today. However, a

53

pancake or waffle sounded appetizing to me too, now that I'd been awake for thirty minutes. I felt guilty having Harriet cooking and waiting on me, but I had to keep reminding myself that this is what I was paying her for—and lodging at the Camelot B&B did not come cheap.

Harriet snubbed out her cigarette, or what little was left of it, and pulled what looked like a turkey platter out of the cabinet. In the wink of an eye she'd placed it before me and instructed me to "chow down."

I sat in mortified silence and stared down at my plate for what must have seemed like a full five minutes to Harriet. Not only had she made me poached eggs on toast again, she had given me twice as much today as she had yesterday.

"Get to eating, girl. Time's a'wasting," she finally said to me. "Since you said ya liked it so much, I gave ya a bit more of it today."

"Horseshit!" Sinbad spat from his cage.

How does that bird read my mind the way he does? If nothing else, it inspired me to get cracking. No more lolling around, reading and procrastinating all day. Time truly was a'wasting.

"Detective Glick will be right with you, ma'am," the bald-headed man at the front desk told me. "He's one of the homicide detectives who was originally assigned to the Pitt case. Please have a seat. It shouldn't be too long."

He turned to a tall, broad man talking on the phone. When he turned back to me I smiled and nodded. He seemed like a nice and pleasant guy. I was relieved, expecting now that all the detectives here would be friendly and accommodating. Earlier, Harriet had given me directions to the Schenectady County sheriff's office on Lafayette Street. I'd hoped for a copy of the original police report, at the very least, and more if I could talk the detective out of additional information.

I waited on a wooden bench for about five minutes until Detective Glick finished his phone call. I watched him as he listened to the caller on the other end of the line. He seemed to respond very infrequently, but roll his eyes often. His was the squarest face I'd ever seen on a human being, almost a Sponge-Bob SquarePants type of face. It was a face that looked as if it had never attempted a smile. He was about my age, and his eyes were nearly the exact color as my own, a light brown resembling cinnamon mixed liberally with sugar—like you'd put on toast if you hadn't already ruined it with runny eggs.

Detective Glick looked like solid muscle poured into a suit. He was a big, broad-shouldered man, six foot six or taller. His hands looked capable of palming a wrecking ball. He glanced my way but didn't acknowledge me. He looked right past me as if I were a fly on the wall. He must not have noticed that this was one of the four and a half days this season that my hair was cooperating. I disliked the detective already.

"Good morning, ma'am," he said, after hanging up the phone. "May I help you? The name's Glick, Ron Glick."

He reminded me of an old rerun I'd watched a few weeks before. The name's Bond, James Bond. Was this Glick guy for real? I half expected him to take off his watch and detonate a bomb with it.

"Nice to meet you, Detective Glick. I'm Lexie Starr," I said, extending my hand in greeting. He ignored my hand, looking as if I were offering him a handful of nuclear waste. Embarrassed, I shoved my hand back into my pocket.

"Step into my office," he commanded. "We'll talk there."

"Thank you for seeing me, detective," I said. We stepped back into his cramped cubicle, which made his immense size seem even more intimidating. "I was hoping you could help me out with a little information about a case from 2001, the Eliza

Pitt murder case. I understand that you were on the investigating team."

He looked surprised at my request. "Why do you want the information, Ms. Starr?" He finally asked.

The Korean-marathoner ploy had worked well before so I tried it again.

"A freelance article?" Glick asked. It was obvious he wasn't buying that story for a second. It irritated me that he would act so distrustful of a liar he'd just met.

"Yes," I said, defiance creeping into my voice.

"You're going to write an article about a case that hasn't even been solved yet?"

"Well, yes. I'm a wr-wr-writer. That's what writers do. They wr-wr-write."

"They wr-wr-write?" Glick asked, imitating my sudden speech impediment.

"Yes, Detective Glick." I was not amused by his mockery. "And I thought I could possibly be of some assistance to you in your investigation. For the sake of my article, of course. Like you said, it would be advantageous to both of us to solve this case."

For someone who couldn't smile, he could laugh quite loud. He acted as if I'd just offered to help him cure cancer, or create world peace. I didn't see any humor in my comment at all. I disliked this man more intensely with each second that passed.

"What I meant to say was, if you could give me what information you have, I'd be happy to share any I have with you too. It's been more than two years since Eliza Pitt was murdered. Frankly, I think you could use a little help solving this one." I nearly sneered at Detective Glick, following my sarcastic jab at his inability to close the case.

"Uh-huh. And what information would you have to share with me, ma'am?"

"Well—er—nothing yet, but . . ."

"Are you willing to testify to that?"

"Well—I—uh . . ."

"Could you sit on the witness stand and explain all that in detail to a panel of jurors?"

Detective Glick was getting as sarcastic as I was, and I didn't like it one little bit. He motioned for me to exit his cubicle, an indication that my five minutes were up. I was being excused. "Listen, ma'am. We're not at liberty to give out confidential information that might jeopardize the investigation—freelance article or not. And actually, this case was recently turned over to the police department in the town where the body was recovered."

"Which was?"

"I'm sorry, ma'am." He stepped away from me and through a door into the men's restroom. Ron Glick wasn't going to be suckered into releasing "classified" information.

Arrogant jerk! His rudeness was inexcusable. I couldn't imagine him treating me with such disparagement because I had no credible information to relay to him. I should have told him that it was "as plain as Harriet's face that it was Eliza's old man that whacked her." They "otter" have known that from the split-lip incident. I was convinced my spunky landlady had more sense than Detective Glick.

I stepped into the phone booth across the street from the sheriff's office and called the number on the card I'd picked up from a holder on Glick's desk. My call was answered on the first ring. I recognized the voice of the bald man at the front desk who had been polite and cooperative earlier. Disguising my voice as best I could, I asked for the records department. He seemed a little confused by my request, but a minute or so later a lady's voice came on the line.

"This is Sandra White. May I help you?"

"Good morning, Sandra," I said. "This is Lydia over at the c-c-county c-c-coroner's office. We received a file today on the Eliza Pitt case that should have been sent to the office currently handling the investigation . . ."

"DeKalb?" she interjected.

"Exactly. Would you have that address handy, S-s-andra?"

"Sure, hang on a minute and I'll get it for you."

EIGHT

"DeKalb, New York—Population 207," the sign read on the outskirts of town. It was a gross exaggeration, I was certain. There couldn't possible be that many inhabitants in this little backwater town, located about an hour north of Schenectady.

The Jeep backfired and began to stall. I stomped on the gas pedal. It sputtered a bit and then picked up speed again. It'd been running perfectly until that moment. I was deep in the Adirondack Mountains by this time and perhaps the four-thousand-foot peak I'd just traversed was playing havoc on the motor. Did carburetors still need "needle valve" adjustments? Maybe I'd recently gotten some bad gasoline in the tank.

I pulled into a gas station to fill up and see if there was anyone there who could look at the motor for me. The only person in the building was a young gal about nineteen who knew even less about car engines than I did. I paid for the gas, bought a Coke, and left. At least I'd made it to DeKalb.

It was easy to find the police station because the entire business district was only two blocks long, including the DeKalb Funeral Home, which took up an entire city block. Apparently people were dying to come to DeKalb. Or more likely, people coming to DeKalb were dying. With a population of 207, they couldn't afford to lose too many more. We'd had more folks than that at our last block party, I'd bet.

I strolled into the tiny police station as if I had a key to the city. I noticed a solitary, and vacant, jail cell in the rear of the room. It was a room that could have been taken from the movie set of *The Andy Griffith Show*. A skinny man, about five foot seven, with slicked-back hair, dressed in a policeman's uniform, was tilted back in a chair with his feet crossed on top of the desk. He quickly jumped up to a standing position when I entered. I introduced myself as Lexie Starr, author, and he introduced himself as Sheriff Wilbur T. Crabb. " 'T' like in Ted," he said, and nearly pumped my arm off in greeting. It felt nice to be so warmly welcomed. I noticed I was getting more comfortable with lying. I hadn't stuttered or examined my nails so far in my conversation with the sheriff.

"So you're Sheriff Wilbur Ted Crabb," I said in a flirtatious manner, trying to win him over into my corner. I'd failed miserably with Detective Glick.

"Oh, no, Ms. Starr. It's Wilbur Tom Crabb."

"Do you go by Wilbur, Will, William, Tom . . . ?"

"I go by Ted," he interrupted.

"I see," I said. "Well, Ted, sir, it's a pleasure to meet you. A good friend of mine, Detective Ron Glick from the Schenectady Homicide Division, told me you were the man to talk to here in DeKalb."

"He did, did he?" Sheriff Crabb puffed up like a tom turkey and hitched up his slacks with his thumbs while he rocked back and forth on the heels and toes of his shoes.

"Yes, he advised me not to talk to anyone else if I wanted to get the straight scoop on the Eliza Pitt case."

"I guess your detective would be right. After all, I am the official authority on the double homicide case now. Eliza Pitt was pregnant, you know. Makes it two murders, you understand." It was clear that Sheriff Crabb was trying to impress me with his knowledge. I pretended to be impressed by his astuteness just to keep him talking.

"Oh, yes, that's good to know, Sheriff Crabb. I can see that

Detective Glick was right. You truly are the man to talk to. You see, I'm writing a novel on the Pitt murder, kind of an Ann Rule–type thing, and I need some information to fill in some gaps in the story," I told him. Freelance article hadn't worked well the last time. I hoped novel might garner a little more respect.

"Well, I'll be hanged. We got us a gen-u-wine, honest-to-goodness author, right here in DeKalb. Wait until my wife hears about this." I had Sheriff Crabb hooked, and it was time to reel him in.

"Now before you get started telling me all you know about the case, Sheriff Crabb, I need to know one more thing. If my publisher were to turn this novel into a movie, to whom should we offer the part of Sheriff Wilbur T. Crabb? Any ideas?"

"Let me think," he said seriously, cupping his chin with his thumb and index finger. "Bruce Willis kind of looks like me, I think. That Rocky feller wouldn't be too bad in the part either, I guess. That Sly guy, you know."

I wrote down in my notebook "Willis, Stallone, Knotts" and wondered to myself, when did Barney Fife get promoted to sheriff?

I spent another hour with Sheriff Crabb. I don't think anyone had trusted the "official authority" with classified information either, and it was easy to understand why. He was anxious to tell me everything he knew about everything—which in the end turned out to be absolutely nothing. When I mentioned Clay's name, Sheriff Crabb asked, "Oh, was he the poor girl's husband? Well, I'll be danged. Say, Ms. Starr, do you reckon they could get heel lifts if they have that Rocky guy play me in the movie? I don't want anyone to think I'm that short. He's a good three or four inches shorter than me, you know." The sheriff squared his bony shoulders and stood up straight to achieve maximum height.

"I'll see to it. I promise." I wondered if the citizens of De-

Kalb slept well at night, knowing this particular lawman was minding the store.

It was evident I was getting nowhere fast with Sheriff Crabb, so I decided to begin my long drive back to the inn. Hopefully my Jeep would make it all the way to Schenectady. I'd run across to the Union Street Diner for a quick bite, and then call it a day. The only useful piece of information I'd extracted from the sheriff was that Rod Crowfoot, the hiker who'd discovered the body, had soon after moved across the country to Seattle. I doubted he had much to offer in the way of information anyway, so I crossed "speak with hiker" off my list.

I bade farewell to the sheriff of DeKalb. He hadn't been particularly informative, but at least he'd been friendly and treated me with a lot more respect that Detective Glick.

I wanted to ask the sheriff if Goober could look at my Jeep before I left.

"Bye now, Ms. Starr," Sheriff Crabb said, through cupped hands.

"Good-bye, and thanks for your help, Sheriff Wilbur 'T like in Ted' Crabb," I shouted out my window as I drove away.

When I sat down to a platter of poached eggs and toast the next morning at six o'clock sharp, I knew I was going to have to come up with a tactful lie. I was getting awfully good at lying by now. It bothered me a bit that it no longer caused me to stutter or feel compelled to crack my knuckles. I hadn't even given my fingernails a second glance in a long while.

"Harriet, your cooking is so terrific that you're turning me into a naughty girl," I said.

Harriet took a deep drag off her Pall Mall and cocked her head in question. "Whatcha talking 'bout, girl?"

"Recently I got a checkup at the health clinic and my cholesterol level was sky high. My triglycerides were off the chart too, and I'd put on ten pounds. I really need to cut back, particularly on the eggs. As much as it pains me, I think I'm going to have to cut out breakfast entirely. That will free you up in the morning anyway."

"But that's what—"

"There's really no sense you cooking just for me," I continued.

"Yeah, but ya know—"

"You have enough to do around here, Harriet, without pampering me."

"But, breakfast's the most 'portant meal of the day. Ain't nobody told ya that?"

"Oh, I know, but skipping breakfast isn't apt to kill me. Got to follow doctor's orders, you know," I said, as I gave Harriet an affectionate wink.

"Bah," she spat. "I ain't been to no doctor in twenty years and look at me. They's all quacks anyway, iffing ya ask me," Harriet said. She patted her mop of white hair, then slid a wooden match across the side of her jeans, lightning fast, and lit another cigarette.

"Well, you're probably right. But just for the heck of it, don't fix me any breakfast from now on. Okay? I'm getting much too fond of your poached eggs, and I don't want to get spoiled to the point that I'll be craving them when I get back home to Kansas."

Harriet brightened at my last comments and nodded. "All righty, girl. Iffing that's what ya want. Price be the same, with or without breakfast, ya know."

"Oh, of course," I said, amused by her spunkiness. After I'd downed another cup of Harriet's gritty coffee, which I was actually beginning to enjoy, I went up to my room to check my e-mail. I had only one message. It was from my extremely enraged and alarmed daughter.

"Where are you?" her message read. "Get in touch with me right now! While I was over at your place, watering your plants, I found Stone Van Patten's number stuck to your computer screen and called him. He wouldn't put you on the phone. Acted like he had no idea where you were, in fact. I'm not sure he even recognized your name. What's going on with you, Mom? This is just not like you at all. If I don't hear from you in the next couple of hours, I'm calling the Myrtle Beach police!"

Oh, goodness. What was I going to do now? I paced around the room frantically and finally decided to walk up and use the pay phone at the drug store up the street. I didn't want Harriet to hear me talking to Wendy, so I couldn't ask to borrow her phone. With any luck at all, Wendy would be too irritated with me to take notice of the area code on her caller ID box.

"Where are you, Mom?" Wendy's voice was anxious.

"I'm right where I said I'd be, honey. To call you, I've had to borrow a cell phone from a gal I've met from New York. What's wrong, Wendy?"

"That man said he couldn't bring you to the phone because you weren't there, hadn't been there, and had no plans of being there as far as he knew."

"Oh, Wendy, I'm s-s-orry. I'll bet you asked for Lexie, didn't you?"

"No, Mom. I asked for Roy Rogers. Of course I asked for Lexie! I told him I was your daughter." Goodness, from who had Wendy inherited her sarcasm?

"Oh, well, that explains it then," I said. "S-s-stone only knows me as Alexandria."

"I asked for Lexie Starr. He doesn't know your last name? Does he have so many girlfriends that he couldn't figure out Lexie was short for Alexandria? Mom, what is going on? And why are you stuttering, by the way?"

"Nothing's going on, Wendy. You know, a lot of gals named

Alexandria go by Alex," I said. Even as I said it, I knew it wasn't going to convince Wendy that Stone had just misunderstood the name. "And I'm not Stone Van Patten's girlfriend. He just seemed like an interesting man when we chatted on the Internet. He doesn't know too much about me. I've been reluctant to share much about myself with a man I hardly know—"

"Like your name?" Wendy interrupted.

"Dear, please settle down. It's nothing like you're imagining. I probably never did think to tell him my last name, or that most people call me Lexie. I haven't even invited Mr. Van Patten to dinner yet, and it's quite likely I won't. I wanted to leave myself free to change my mind about meeting him. So, you see, he was being quite truthful when he told you he was unaware of my plans. Meeting Mr. Van Patten is not my main concern, just something I thought I'd consider while I was out here. I spent the first couple days driving around New England, enjoying the fall colors. Then I drove down the coastline to South Carolina. Now I'm in Myrtle Beach and I plan to spend a few days shopping. I thought maybe I could get my Christmas shopping done early, and there are some wonderful shops here on the Grand Strand." Good grief, what a liar I'd become!

"The what?"

"It's what they call the main stretch through town," I said. "It's a strip of land between the inter-coastal waterway, in this case the Waccamaw River, and the Atlantic Ocean. There are a lot of shops along the 'strand' and good seafood restaurants too."

I didn't know what I was talking about, but I thought I'd distract Wendy with a couple of details that I could recall from one of Stone's e-mails. "I've eaten so many crabs that I'm about to turn into one, I think."

I was more apt to turn into a poached egg, actually. But I did meet a Crabb—Wilbur T. Crabb, to be exact. The slivers of truth in my statements were getting harder and harder to detect. "When are you coming home, Mom?" Wendy obviously didn't care that I was turning into a crab. She was probably more concerned I might be turning into a blooming idiot.

"I don't know, honey. When I've seen all I want to see, I suppose. Why were you trying to get in touch with me in the first place? Is something wrong?"

"No, Clay and I just had some good news for you. I was too excited to wait for you to come home, so I thought I'd call and tell you on the phone."

Dread settled into the pit of my stomach. "So tell me, honey, what's the good news?"

"You're going to be a grandmother!" Wendy practically shrieked into the phone. "Sometime around the end of May."

"Oh Wendy—how wonderful!" I said. Oh, Wendy, how terrible, I thought. "When you get further along, are you going to try to find out what gender it is?"

"I haven't decided if I want to know yet. I'm kind of hoping our first child is a boy—but I really don't care one way or the other. Although, I'd imagine knowing in advance would make it easier to decorate the nursery."

"Well, I don't care whether it's a boy or a girl, either, as long as it's healthy. I'm thrilled for both of you—and me too, of course. My first grandchild—imagine that! I'll bet Clay is as excited as we are," I said. I was going out on a fishing expedition.

"Oh, I'm sure he will be, once he gets used to the idea of being a father," she replied after a short hesitation. I thought I was getting a nibble.

"Clay does want children, doesn't he?" I needed just a tad more bait on the hook.

"Yeah, sure, of course he does," Wendy said, and laughed in a nervous reaction to my question. "He just doesn't know it yet."

Now that was definitely a bite! My fishing trip had been successful. I'd found out what I wanted to know. Wendy's response told me Clay was not happy about having another pregnant wife on his hands. Now I knew I had to do something to get my daughter away from this man, and do it soon. When his first wife became pregnant, she ended up dead. I couldn't stand by and allow this same fate to befall Wendy.

We spoke for a few more minutes. Before I hung up I asked her if she still had Mr. Van Patten's number handy. I didn't have it with me, and I was going to have to call him and try to explain my daughter's frantic phone call to him. Besides, it might help convince Wendy that Stone and I weren't involved in some hot and heavy, clandestine affair. I'd surely know his phone number if that were the case.

"I've got to go, honey. I need to get this phone back to the nice lady I borrowed it from. I won't be out here too much longer, and we'll talk more about the baby when I get back. Okay? I love you, Wendy."

"I love you too, Mom. Promise me you'll be careful."

"You know I will. Don't you worry."

"Well, all right. I'll try not to worry. Keep in touch."

"I will. Bye-bye now, Wendy."

"Bye, Mom."

NINE

"Mr. Van Patten?" I spoke, hesitantly, into the pay phone.

"Yes, this is he."

"This is Lexie Starr. You're working on locating charms for a bracelet for me."

"Of course, Lexie. Where are you? I had a hysterical phone call from your daughter yesterday, and I've been worried sick about you since. She caught me off guard, and I'm afraid I only made her more concerned."

What a sweet man, I thought. He was worried sick about me and we'd never even met. It felt kind of nice to have a man concerned about my well-being.

"Oh, well, er—Mr. Van Patten—"

"It's Stone—"

"Stone. It's a very long, rather embarrassing story and—"

"Go on—"

"Well, you see, to protect her from knowing too much, I had to tell my daughter that I was going to Myrtle Beach to meet you. Remember you offered to be my tour guide and all? The leaves are all so pretty back here this time of year. And the crabs are good too, I'm sure." I was floundering, humiliated to the bone, and probably making no sense at all. I felt as if I was beginning to hyperventilate and feared I'd soon need to breathe into a brown paper bag. "But to make a long story short, Stone, I'm just fine."

"That much is a relief. I'm not sure I understood the rest of what you said, but I think I'd like to hear all the details. And, of course, the tour guide offer still stands."

"Well, actually I'm not in Myrtle Beach at all. I'm in Schenectady, New York."

"Now I think I'd really enjoy hearing all the details." He laughed pleasantly into the phone. "Say, a thought just occurred to me. I've got to fly up to New York City in a couple of days. I need to pick up some diamonds at a shop up there. I'll have a rental car and some spare time before my return flight. Any possibility of meeting me for lunch one day this week? I'll book my flight for whatever day works for you. I'm flexible on which day I pick up my diamond order. If we meet for lunch, you'll be able to explain it all to me then. I sincerely would like to meet you, Ms. Starr."

"Have lunch with a guy hauling a load of diamonds around with him? How could I pass up an offer like that? Diamonds are a girl's best friend, you know." And for some reason, I really wanted someone to hear my ideas who might offer suggestions and opinions. I'd welcome someone to talk to, someone with whom I could share my concerns. Perhaps then I wouldn't feel so overwhelmed by trying to tackle all this alone. Stone seemed like just the type of person I was visualizing.

Stone laughed again at my comment about girls loving diamonds. He asked me to take the ferry to Liberty Island on Thursday morning, and he'd meet me at the top of the Statue of Liberty at eleven o'clock. I told him I'd never been there before, and he insisted that no trip to New York was complete without a visit to the statue. He'd pick up something at a nearby deli on the way. We could talk and have a picnic on the grounds of Liberty Island. It sounded like fun to me, and I was looking forward to Thursday. I sincerely hoped he was as nice a guy in person as he seemed on the phone. Of course, Ted Bundy could have easily charmed a lady into meeting him on Liberty Island too. Oh, goodness, I thought. What had I gotten myself into?

As Wendy had said, I didn't know him from Adam. When I expressed concern about how I'd recognize him in a crowd of strangers, he said, "I'll be the one wearing a T-shirt that says, 'Myrtle Beach is for Lovers.' Will that work?"

I blushed. I was thankful he couldn't see my reaction to his remark over the phone. "I guess that'll work," I said, and chuckled nervously. "See you at eleven on Thursday, Stone."

I spent the next few days at the Schenectady Public Library on Clinton Street, on one of their computers, searching through databases of old editions of the local newspapers. I also searched again through the microfilm I'd borrowed from the library where I volunteered my services, in case I'd overlooked something about the case. I didn't find out much, but I hoped what little I did discover might prove useful at some point.

One article mentioned that since the murder of his wife, Clayton had been staying in Boston with a friend, Jake Jacoby, during the week, and returning home to New York on weekends. It was too far to commute to the police academy in Boston each day. Clay had told the reporter it was hard enough to go home to an empty house on Friday nights.

Clay claimed to be at a library in Boston, studying by himself, on the day Eliza disappeared. So far no one had come forward to substantiate that claim other than Jacoby, whose credibility was also questionable. That answered one of my questions—Clay had moved from the Boston motel to his friend's house after Eliza's death. Only on weekends did he travel back to his home in Schenectady.

Another article mentioned that when the hiker, Rod Crowfoot, had stumbled across the body some twenty feet off a hiking trail in the Adirondacks, there'd been a thirty-aught-six cartridge found near the crime scene, although there were no bullet wounds in the body. The authorities had yet to determine if the high-powered rifle cartridge was connected in any way to the murder, or murderer.

One last bit of information gleaned from the newspaper articles was that Eliza's car was found in the Food Pantry's parking lot with several bags of groceries in the trunk. A young employee of the grocery store, Kale Miller, had carried the bags to her car, placed them in her trunk, and headed back into the store. According to Kale, Mrs. Pitt was rearranging the contents of her trunk as he walked away from her. He didn't recall anyone else in the parking lot, but admitted he hadn't been paying much attention at the time. Eliza apparently had been abducted from the parking lot after she'd closed the trunk, and before she'd gotten into the car.

I made photocopies of every article I could find about the case and stored them in my notebook. I promised myself I'd go about this impromptu investigation in an organized manner, even though "organized" was not one of my natural traits. So far, so good, I thought.

The rest of my spare time was spent reading and relaxing on Harriet's back porch. I had found another little diner, several blocks west of the Camelot B&B, which served sourdough English muffins for breakfast. I went there each morning, and to the Union Street Diner for supper.

I had fallen into a comfortable routine. Harriet usually joined me on the back porch in the evenings for a quick chat. She allowed herself about ten minutes of downtime each day. She'd sit on her rusty bucket and smoke three cigarettes in ten minutes before rushing off to tackle another chore.

During her ten-minute break on Wednesday evening, I asked her about her family. She told me she had one son living in Schenectady, and another son in Florida. Her husband had been killed in a boating mishap when her boys were both in high school. He was drunk one day, Harriet said, and capsized his fishing boat by running it into a submerged log. Her husband drowned when the boat sank to the bottom of the lake.

"Oh, Harriet, I'm so sorry. That was really a terrible tragedy," I said.

"Yeah, it shore were," she said and nodded. "It were a brand-spanking-new boat."

TEN

I crawled out of bed early on Thursday morning, even earlier than Harriet. I knew it'd take me a while to drive to Battery Park in New York. From there I planned to take the ferry across to Liberty Island. I preferred to get there a bit early and wait for Stone than to get there late and have him waiting for me. I wasn't familiar with New York or the traffic there, so I didn't know with any degree of accuracy how to estimate the time it would take to drive there.

Since my four and a half days were up on my fuss-free hairstyle, I had to spend a good twenty minutes with the curling iron. Then I had to spend another ten or fifteen minutes changing into every outfit I'd brought with me before finally settling on the first outfit I'd tried on. The thought occurred to me that getting back into the dating scene required almost more time and trouble than I was prepared to sacrifice.

I bypassed my morning English muffin since we'd have an early lunch and I didn't want to run the risk of arriving late. Not to mention I was leaving Schenectady in what seemed like the middle of the night. As it turned out, I got turned around a couple of times in New York City, driving through a tunnel three times before I recognized it as the same Holland Tunnel I'd already passed through twice before. I finally arrived at Battery Park at about ten-twenty-five. I paid the ten-dollar fee to take the ten-thirty ferry across to the island. Crossing over to the island on the ferry, I overheard two young women chatting.

One of them remarked, "Too bad we can't go up in the statue." I wondered why they couldn't. Neither one of them looked to be handicapped.

I found out soon enough that no one could go up in the statue. It'd been closed to tourists since the September eleventh terrorist attacks in 2001. Because of the mob of people milling about the grounds, I wondered whether I'd even find Stone. I was too vain to wear my glasses, so I'd left them in my car's glove compartment. Now I had to get within about ten feet of a fellow to read the front of his T-shirt. I walked around for forty-five minutes staring at every man's chest that drew near me.

I glanced at my watch and saw that it was already almost noon. Would Stone wait for me or had he left? I wondered. Maybe he'd decided I'd stood him up when I didn't appear at eleven. Then again, maybe he had stood me up! I didn't think he'd do something that inconsiderate. From what little I knew of him, it didn't seem his style at all. Mine, maybe, but not Stone's.

I was just about to sit down on a nearby bench and sob when I felt a gentle tap on my shoulder. "Are you Lexie Starr?" I heard a soft-spoken voice ask. I recognized the voice from our previous phone conversation and breathed a huge sigh of relief.

"Yes. Stone?"

"Uh-huh," he replied with a nod. He gave me a brief, casual embrace. "I was beginning to think we wouldn't be able to find each other in this swarm of people. You were standing there alone and looking as frustrated as I felt, so I took a chance and approached you. I'm sorry, I had no idea they hadn't reopened the statue to visitors since the nine-eleven attacks. I did manage to find a little out-of-the-way corner for us to have lunch. No picnic tables, but I guess we can make do with a bench."

With his arm draped loosely over my shoulder, he led me to the spot he'd found. As he unloaded a bag of sandwiches, cheese slices, grapes, and Diet Cokes, I checked him out as best I could without being obvious. I had to smile at his silly-looking Myrtle Beach T-shirt. He obviously had a fun sense of humor.

Stone wasn't a tall man, maybe five foot nine or ten, but he was still over a half-foot taller than I was. He carried an extra ten or fifteen pounds around his waist that I found rather comforting. Better to look slim next to a chunky guy than chunky next to a slim guy, I've always thought. His silver hair was fashionably cut and just beginning to recede a little on top. He had the lightest blue eyes I've ever seen, so light they were almost translucent. I felt that if I looked straight into Stone's eyes, I'd be able to see through the irises to a bank of information behind them. He spoke in an intelligent, articulate manner.

Stone also had a very small gap between his two front teeth, which were otherwise straight and extremely white. I thought he was one of the most handsome men I'd ever met. I thought this right after he commented that I was even prettier in person than I'd sounded on the phone. And younger than he'd anticipated. He said, "I would have guessed you'd be in your mid-forties, but you can't be out of your thirties yet." Right, Stone, I thought. And I can't be more than a hundred pounds, soaking wet, either. One of the things that impressed me most about Stone, aside from his expressions of adulation, was the fact that he was an excellent listener. Between bites of my lunch, I found myself telling him about my late husband, my daughter, my son-in-law, and my volunteer service at the library.

Eventually I explained the situation that had brought me back East to begin with and that had prompted the frantic phone call he'd received from Wendy. I even told him about my aversion to poached eggs and my allergies to bee stings and pork. He seemed so sincerely interested in everything I had to say that I couldn't prevent myself from talking incessantly. It never occurred to me that a near stranger couldn't seriously care about my tendency to swell up like a hot air balloon after ingesting a pork chop.

Now and then, when I stopped to breathe, I learned an interesting tidbit about Stone, as well. He told me he was fifty-five and widowed. Having both lost our spouses was something we had in common, he pointed out. He was financially able to retire, but was afraid he wouldn't know what to do with himself if he didn't have a job to go to each day. He wasn't a man who welcomed idle time, he said.

He'd never taken the time to cultivate any hobbies, to speak of; he didn't golf, fish, collect anything, or do woodworking. He read quite a bit, but he seldom watched television. I tried to visualize a man without an intense attachment to his remote control. Stone explained how he'd concentrated on his work the last few years. His wife, Diana, had been diagnosed with ovarian cancer shortly after they were married, and the necessary hysterectomy had prevented them from ever having children. The disease had come back in the form of colon cancer about six years ago, and he'd lost his partner of twenty-seven years. I could tell that he and Diana had shared a close and special relationship by the tenderness in his voice as he spoke of her.

After her death he'd moved into a small apartment in Myrtle Beach. He'd felt like he was rattling around in the large home they'd shared, and the home was too full of memories of Diana. To preserve his sanity, he'd chosen to relocate.

Stone's father had been a jeweler by trade, and Stone had followed in his footsteps, eventually taking over ownership of Pawley's Island Jewelers when his father was stricken with Alzheimer's disease. His father now resided in an extended-care facility and Stone visited him as often as he could, even though his dad no longer recognized him most of the time. His mother had passed away a couple of years prior with heart failure. He was close to both his sister and brother and their families. Stone was particularly fond of his thirty-two-year-old nephew, Andrew, or Andy to his family and friends. Stone, by the way, was Stone's actual given name, he said. Because his father was also a jeweler, this name was perfectly logical to me. Stone's siblings, Sterling and Jewel, also had jewelry-related monikers. Jewel lived in North Carolina with her husband, Brady, who was a postal employee.

Two men worked for him at the jewelry store—Jack Weber and Lance Steiner. Lance wanted to purchase the business from Stone in about two years, and was saving money and building up a down payment in the meantime. Stone had offered to carry the mortgage when the time came to transfer ownership of the jewelry store. In just the last year or so, Stone had reformatted the business so that it was strictly an online jewelry source. He felt it gave him greater flexibility, and was less confining.

Before we knew it, several hours had passed. Stone knew I wanted to drive back to Schenectady before it grew dark, so he recommended that we catch the next ferry back to Battery Park. He paid for the two tickets and escorted me to a seat on the return ferry.

"Lexie, forgive me if I'm being too forward or presumptuous. I've really enjoyed myself today," Stone said.

"I have too. These last few hours have been delightful. And you aren't being too presumptuous at all."

"Well, I haven't actually got to the presumptuous part yet," he said good-naturedly.

"Oh," I said. "Then hurry up and get to it."

He laughed at my impatience and continued. "With Lance and Jack at the store I can get away about any time I want now. I think they actually prefer to have me out from under their feet as much as possible. I really need a break from the business too. I've gotten into a monotonous rut, I'm afraid.

"So, Lexie, I was thinking of getting away from Myrtle Beach for a while. If Harriet has a room available at the inn, I could rent it and spend a week or two helping you with your investigation. Only, of course, if you'd welcome the company. I'd enjoy the time with you, and I'd feel better knowing that you weren't tackling all this by yourself. You are involved in something that could become dangerous, you know."

"I don't think I'm apt to try anything too courageous or fraught with peril, but I'd be very appreciative of your company. Maybe an extra head at this point would be beneficial too. You might think of something that I'm not smart enough to think of or am just overlooking."

"So you don't think that's being too presumptuous?"

"Of course I do, Stone, and I adore you for it! I do know for a fact that Harriet has vacancies. I'm her only lodger at the moment. How do you feel about poached eggs on toast at six in the morning?"

He chuckled, and said, "I may have to come up with an allergy myself. I'm deathly allergic to eggs and getting up before seven a.m. gives me a migraine. How does that sound?"

"That just might work. But if you need any help lying, just ask, and I'll give you some pointers," I replied. "Although you did do pretty well with that 'you can't be out of your thirties' thing. Oh, and be prepared for an African gray parrot to swear at you every time you walk into Harriet's kitchen."

ELEVEN

After drinking several cups of Harriet's coffee on Friday morning, I checked my e-mail and found I had two messages. The first one was from Stone saying it hadn't taken long at all to tie up loose ends, like packing, changing the oil in his car, and notifying Lance Steiner that he'd be taking some time off. Stone would be arriving in Schenectady about six o'clock in the evening, if all went as planned.

"Let's have dinner after I arrive," Stone suggested.

The other message was from Wendy. It was filled with chitchat and gossip and ended with a note of admonishment. "I hope you are using a little judgment and caution. Not everyone is as they appear to be."

"Not everyone is as they appear to be." Eight words of extremely good advice, I'd have to admit. In fact, those eight words pretty much summed up the reason that I was currently holed up in a bed and breakfast in New York.

I sent a quick reply, assuring Wendy that I would be careful. I didn't want her worrying about me, so I indicated in my message that there was a very good chance that I would opt not even to invite Stone to have supper with me.

"I'm enjoying myself," I wrote. "I just needed to get away for a little while. I'll probably decide not to complicate matters by meeting Mr. Van Patten, at all. So, you see, there is really no reason for you to be concerned."

After I'd logged off the Internet, I was antsy and restless. I decided to burn off some of my excess energy by walking up the street for an English muffin. It was a beautiful morning, and the exercise would be good for me.

I didn't see one empty table when I stepped into the little café. I wasn't anxious to sit next to a stranger, nor did I want to stand around and wait for a table to open up. I kept walking down Union Street, turned left at the next intersection, headed south on Fourteenth Street, and before I knew it, I was walking past the Food Pantry grocery store where Eliza Pitt was last seen on April 12, 2001.

I walked into the store and wandered around, searching for the bakery department. A few minutes later I approached the checkout stand with a chocolate long john and a Diet Coke. I had theorized that the Diet Coke would cancel out the calories in the doughnut. I knew it didn't actually work that way, but it allowed me to enjoy the doughnut without guilt. As the cashier counted out my change, I thought back to the article I'd read earlier and tried to conjure up the name of the store's sacker who'd accompanied Eliza to the parking lot the day she disappeared.

After I paid the cashier, I casually asked, "Is Kyle here today, by any chance?"

"Kyle? Do you mean Kale?" the young female clerk replied. "Kale Miller?"

"Yes, that's who I meant, Kale Miller."

"No, ma'am. They let Kale go about a year ago, just a month or so after I started working here."

"Oh? Why'd they let him go? He seemed like such a nice young man whenever he loaded my groceries into my car for me."

"Yeah, I guess Kale was nice enough, but several customers complained to the manager about him. At least that's what I heard. He'd had one of his epileptic fits a few days before he was fired—he was epileptic, you know—"

"Uh-huh. Yes, uh, of course."

"But I really don't think that had anything to do with his getting fired."

"I wouldn't think so."

I thanked the young girl, walked outside to eat my doughnut, and gave some thought to what I'd just learned. I finished the pastry, tossed the wax paper tissue into the trash receptacle outside the store, and walked back into the Food Pantry. This time I headed straight for the customer service desk in the rear of the store.

"Is the manager in today?" I asked the man behind the counter.

He nodded, picked up the phone and spoke into it before pointing me back to a small office next to the employee restroom.

"Good morning. May I help you?" A pleasant, rosy-faced man, about my age, greeted me as he stood up behind his desk.

"Good morning. I'm Doctor Thelma Roush," I said.

"Nice to meet you, Doctor Roush. I'm Charlie Hickman. What can I do for you?"

"It's nice to meet you too. I'm with the research department at the hospital. I'm in charge of a team that's currently testing a new drug to help control epilepsy—we call it CT-43. 'CT' stands for clinical trial, of course."

"Okay, but—"

"I'm sure you're wondering what all this has to do with you?"

"Yes, as a matter of fact."

"Well, actually, it has to do with a former employee of yours, Kale Miller. He's epileptic, you know."

"Yes, I was aware of that, Doctor Roush."

"Then you were probably also aware that he was involved in

this clinical trial, testing the new drug, CT-43, for FDA approval."

I really had no idea how new drugs were approved, but I doubted that the Food Pantry manager was familiar with the procedure either.

"No, I didn't know anything about Kale being involved in your clinical trial. But he hasn't been employed here for about a year, so I won't be able to help you."

"Do you know where I can locate Kale?"

"No. I think he still lives with his folks over on Terrace Lane, but I'm not certain."

"The problem is that Kale hasn't shown up for his last couple of appointments. Because of the potential side effects of any newly developed pharmaceutical product, he needs to be closely monitored. We're particularly concerned about the possibility of arrhythmia, abnormal heart palpitations, and liver damage."

Charlie seemed impressed with my knowledge and professionalism. I was impressed, myself, that I could come up with words like "pharmaceutical" and "arrhythmia" at the drop of a hat.

While I let Charlie absorb the seriousness of the situation, I continued, "Can you tell me why Kale is no longer employed at the Food Pantry? Was he exhibiting unpleasant side effects or having frequent epileptic seizures?"

"Actually, he did have a seizure not long before we had to let him go."

I shook my head in dismay. This was obviously not good news for the future of the drug, CT-43. And that, naturally, was my main concern as far as Charlie was concerned.

"Why was he let go? Do you mind sharing that with me?"

"Oh, it had nothing to do with his epilepsy, Doctor Roush," he said. "We'd had several complaints that Kale was making some of our female customers uncomfortable."

"How was he doing that, may I ask?"

"He was insisting on carrying their bags out, even when they had requested to do it themselves. Then he apparently propositioned a few of them outside the store."

"Was he showing an indication of aggression toward them? Another potential side effect, I'm afraid," I said, in my best physician's voice.

"No, not really, doctor. It wasn't like he was accosting them in the parking lot or anything of that nature. It was more of an overly flirtatious manner than aggression. He's basically just a harmless young guy, with a tendency to be a little too forward at times. Well, I'm sure you know how it is with Kale."

"Of course."

"I spoke to him several times about it, and yet he continued to make unwelcome advances to the ladies. Kale's a good kid, with a lot of strikes against him, so I hated to let him go. But I couldn't have him distressing my customers, as I'm sure you can understand. Keeping my head above water—with that new market over on Twelfth Street, and all—is tough enough without having problems like that."

"Of course," I said again.

"I'm sure it had nothing to do with your CT-43 drug, Doctor Roush. If anything, it probably had more to do with that schizophrenia he was diagnosed with last year."

Schizophrenia? Oh good grief, I thought, as I left the Food Pantry. I pondered the implications as I walked back toward the Camelot B&B. Could one of Kale's multiple personalities be that of a harmless flirt, and another one a homicidal maniac? Had he been thoroughly investigated by the authorities? I came to the conclusion that it wouldn't hurt to check it out. I stopped at a pay phone outside a convenience store, removed Detective

Glick's business card from my fanny pack, and dialed his number.

"Detective Glick." I heard his voice on the handset.

"Good morning, detective. This is Lexie Starr again. I have some information that might possibly have some bearing on the Eliza Pitt case."

"And what would that be, Ms. Starr?" he asked, with a lot of impatience, and a touch of annoyance in his tone.

"Are you aware that Kale Miller, the sacker at Food—"

"I know who he is," Detective Glick cut in.

"—Pantry, suffers from schizophrenia?"

"Yes, I'm aware of that discovery."

"Oh. Well, did you consider all the ramifications of that discovery?"

"As much as we felt necessary," he said. "Have a good day, Ms. Starr."

Unfortunately, Detective Glick had disconnected the call before I could respond and slam the phone down in his ear.

"Arrogant jerk!" I said into the phone anyway. At least I had found out that Kale's affliction had been scrutinized to the satisfaction of the homicide detectives. I'd have to be content knowing that the team of investigators felt Kale Miller was un-involved in the disappearance and murder of Eliza Pitt. And it didn't hurt to let Detective Glick know that I was still on the case, despite his lack of cooperation and his condescending at-titude.

TWELVE

Stone registered for the room down the hall from me early Friday evening. I'm not sure what reason he gave Harriet for not wanting any morning meals cooked for him, but from the top of the stairs I heard Harriet respond, "Price be the same, with or without breakfast, ya know." I then heard Stone chuckle and agree. I smiled to myself at the exchange. I'd warned him of Harriet's eccentric, but enchanting, personality.

Stone's room had its own bathroom, which was a great relief to me. After an offhand remark he'd made Thursday about my "natural beauty," I didn't want him to see how much paraphernalia, and how many potions, it took to look this naturally beautiful. I had toiletries strung from one end of my bathroom to the other. Stone was a flatterer, or possibly just a gifted BS'er, but he knew how to make a woman feel good about herself. I was eating up the praise and attention, and I'm the first to admit that I was enjoying it.

After Stone settled into his room, the two of us walked across the street to the Union Street Diner for supper. At our table in the corner, Stone admitted that he needed to drop a little weight, and I told him that I also had picked up some extra, unwanted pounds.

"You look to me to be at your ideal weight, Lexie. Where are you hiding these unwanted pounds?"

"You're just being kind, Stone. I can tell you're a real charmer and have no reservations about lying through your teeth. Please, don't let me stop you."

He looked at me with a feigned expression of having wounded feelings, then pointed to his mouth, and said, "See this gap? It'd make it easy to lie through my teeth, if I wanted to. But I mean everything I say, my dear."

"You're a smooth one, aren't you, Stone? Remind me to be wary of you."

"No need for that—say, how 'bout we share an order of chicken and dumplings? Then we needn't feel as guilty about all the fat and cholesterol we're devouring."

While we waited on the chicken and dumplings, we talked about Schenectady. We discussed how friendly the people seemed to be, and how nice and clean the city appeared. A couple of local men, both dressed in insulated coveralls, chatted with us for a few minutes. One of them asked where we hailed from and why we were visiting the area. I told them that we were investigating the 2001 Pitt murder case for a potential novel I was thinking about penning. I wanted to stay consistent with my story.

"Good luck," one of the men said as he fished change out of his pocket before heading for the cash register. Then he turned, paused and said, "Hard to imagine that anyone could bludgeon his pregnant wife to death with a rock, isn't it?"

Stone raised his eyebrows and held my gaze. I realized then that this was the first time I'd heard how Eliza had been murdered. I'd assumed that she was shot, stabbed, or choked to death. Not that any one of them was less vicious than the other options. It was obvious that many of the locals believed Clay was the culprit. I shuddered and wondered how Wendy could be attracted to someone cruel enough to do such a thing. If he did such a thing, I stopped to remind myself.

I also wondered how Clay was accepting her pregnancy. Was he already plotting Wendy and the baby's demise? Why would he want to be shackled to this child any more than the one Eliza was carrying, if and when he killed her?

After supper, Stone and I went into the hardware store next to the diner. He bought a comfortable canvas lawn chair for Harriet's back porch. Like me, Stone wanted to have a place to read and relax on the porch in the evenings. And, I suspected, to be near me at the same time. I'd shown him the five-hundred-pound pumpkin in the backyard, the hanging chair that I was so enthralled with, and also Harriet's metal bucket. He said he couldn't see himself being comfortable on a bucket that was apt to collapse into a pile of rusty scrap metal beneath him, and he didn't dare sit in my beloved chair.

"That would be about as hazardous as petting a baby moose with the mother moose standing twenty feet away," Stone said.

I laughed and agreed, and then thought about the moose head that had appeared in Clay and Wendy's den.

"Speaking of moose, Stone, do you know where a person in this region could go to shoot one?"

"You have a sudden desire to go out and pop a moose?" he asked.

"No, you nincompoop," I said, and smacked his shoulder playfully. "I'm wondering where a hunter—not me—might shoot one around here."

"Legally?"

"Not necessarily."

"Well, I just happened to have read an article about that recently. It said there are a guesstimated one hundred moose in the Adirondack Mountain Range right now, and the population is growing. There's no active program here of tagging moose in order to learn more about them or to keep track of their numbers. But it's a protected species in New York, so there's no season on them. They're working hard to bring the moose back to the Adirondacks in more impressive numbers. Poaching one in New York carries a maximum sentence of two thousand dollars and/or a year in jail. Why do you ask?"

"Oh, I was just curious. Clay brought a mounted bull moose head back to Kansas from here, and I was wondering where he might have bagged it."

"He could have shot it legally in Vermont where there are about four thousand moose. More moose are killed in traffic accidents in Vermont each year than those that make their home in this state. Do you know if he ever went hunting in Vermont?"

"No, but I suppose it's possible. Anyway, thanks for the info. It's going to be nice having you here to assist me. For the moral support alone, not to mention off-the-wall information such as the wildlife population of Vermont. You moose be very smart, Stone."

"Yes, I moose be."

There was frost on Harriet's pumpkin when we awoke Saturday morning. It was a reminder that winter was just around the corner. I was in my newly designated favorite chair on the back porch, Lady Luck coffee cup in my hand, when Stone walked out with his own steaming cup. He was spitting coffee grounds out as he walked toward the new canvas chair he'd purchased. "Remind me to buy some toothpicks, will you, Lexie?"

I laughed at his remark. "Give it a week. It'll grow on you. Trust me."

"Are you telling me that this coffee has already been brewing for a week?" he asked. "Hmmm. I'd expected as much. Not that I'm complaining, mind you. I needed a jump start this morning. I can't remember the last time I slept so soundly."

"Those featherbed mattresses are heavenly, aren't they? This place seems to me to be the perfect example of why we should all go back to more traditional, old-fashioned customs. These days, everything tends to be too technical, too cold and impersonal. Life was simpler, and more satisfying, back in the good old days."

Stone agreed. His room at the inn featured a four-poster bed like mine, except his had no canopy, and the bedspread was more masculine, with large colorful wood ducks appliquéd across a solid white background. Like mine, his room had wall-to-wall throw rugs and an antique dresser with candles on either side of a large oval mirror. The colors in his bathroom were a bit subtler than those in mine, but not by much.

"Just walking into your bathroom ought to be enough to wake you up," I said. "I was afraid to walk into mine after eating Harriet's poached eggs. Thought it could be just enough to upset the apple cart, if you know what I mean."

"Yes, I do know what you mean. At first glance, the color schemes here are nearly overwhelming. She's one in a million, though—our Harriet," Stone said. "By the way, did you happen to see what she keeps in the bookcase in the family room?"

"No, what?"

"Well, books of course—"

"Books?" I cut in. "No kidding? Gee, that's odd. I wouldn't think even Harriet would keep books in a bookcase."

"Not just regular books, though. Mostly phone books. Stacks of them. Every Schenectady phone book from 1957 through the 2003 edition that just came out this year."

"Okay, now that is a bit odd. But for Harriet, maybe it's not really all that shocking."

"Good point. Since I was up early this morning, I looked through a number of them, just for the heck of it," Stone said. "The hiker who discovered Eliza's body, Rod Crowfoot, is listed in the 2001 phone book, but none of them before or after that. It shows his address as 1022 Huron Street, Apartment C. That's just a few blocks from here. I thought we ought to run by there this morning. I would imagine that after Rod discovered the body, he was talking about it to about everyone he ran into. That'd be the natural thing to do, after all. He may have relayed some useful information to the super, the maintenance man, or gardener at the apartment complex."

"Couldn't hurt to stop by there and ask around, could it? Want to stop and get an English muffin for breakfast on the way?"

"No, I want to stop and get a bacon and cheese omelet, hash browns, biscuits and gravy, and a cinnamon roll, but I guess an English muffin will have to suffice."

I patted his slightly protruding belly, surprised at the affection I already felt for him. He was such an easy, comfortable guy to have around. I thanked God one more time that Stone had volunteered to accompany me in Schenectady.

"Maybe a cinnamon roll instead of an English muffin will be okay, just this once," I said. "But no biscuits and gravy. Too much cholesterol. So, Harriet's really kept all of the phone books since 1957?"

"Don't really know much about that Crowfoot guy. Doubt anyone around here knows much. Least nothing that will be of any use for your novel," Fred, the toothless guy behind the desk, told us. I was still using my "novel" approach, although I doubted Fred was a voracious reader. I listened as he leaned back in his chair and told us what he remembered about the former tenant.

"Kid didn't socialize much. Kept to himself most the time. Was only in his apartment once that I recall. Had a toilet that wouldn't flush worth a damn—excuse me—hoot, I mean." Fred looked at me in silent apology and kept talking.

"Think he's Native American. Couldn't tell you what tribe he belongs to. I'd guess his mother was white, his daddy Indian.

Looked mostly white to me." Because of the missing teeth, Fred talked with a slight lisp that made him sound like a cartoon character.

"Do you know where he worked?" Stone asked.

"Was working at a local seafood restaurant. Washing dishes, last I heard. Tended to go from job to job. Never seemed to work at any one place for more than a month or two. Was bussing tables, or something, for a while at the Starlight Lounge. Joint's right down the street. Don't know what, but something happened and he got canned."

I noticed that Fred didn't waste a lot of time on personal pronouns. Between the lisp and the choppy speech pattern, I had to concentrate to keep up with what he was saying.

"After he discovered Eliza Pitt's body, did he talk about it any?" Stone asked.

"Not that I recall. Not even to the media. Followed him around like he was the Pied Piper," Fred said. "Never talked much to anybody about anything. Like I said, he kept to himself. Moved right after that, anyway. Back to Washington. Did hear tell that he spent a lot of his childhood in foster homes. Got moved from place to place. Finally stayed in the last one for several years. Can't remember who told me that. Don't think it was Rod. He never spoke about much of anything. But I do know he'd been real fond of those foster parents. Spoke of them quite often. Referred to that foster father as Uncle Bill. But Uncle Bill apparently died right before Rod moved here. Kid seemed like a lost soul to me."

"Did Rod go hiking in the mountains a lot?" Stone asked.

"Don't really know. Might have. Wasn't around a whole lot on weekends. Didn't particularly seem like the hiker type to me. Too lazy to pick his own nose, if you want to know the truth. That's why he couldn't hold a job for long. Do know that he must've spent a lot of his spare time hunting for unusual hatpins. Always wore one of those fishing-type hats. Must've had at least fifty hatpins attached to it. After he moved out, I found two of them on the floor of his apartment. One was a Seattle Supersonics pin from 1979. Won the NBA Finals that year. Other one was an apple that had 'I love New York' across it."

"Just something to show where he's been, I suppose, like a charm bracelet," I said, more to myself than anyone else. "Do you know why he moved to Seattle, Fred?"

"Born and raised there. Didn't like it here, I guess. Moved back to where he come from. Like everyone else seems to do eventually."

We stopped at the Starlight Lounge for lunch. It was a bar and grill, so we ordered hamburgers and beer. Like myself, Stone occasionally liked a cold one with lunch, so we thought we'd try a pale ale they had on tap that came from a local microbrewery.

"Say, son, do you remember anything about an Indian guy named Rod Crowfoot that used to work here for a short spell back in 2001?" Stone asked the waiter.

"No, sorry sir. I just started here last month. But Bernie, the cook, might remember him. He's been working here for years. I'll ask him and let you know," the young man offered.

"Thanks, I'd sure appreciate it."

About halfway through our sandwiches, the waiter came back and told us what the cook had said. "Bernie doesn't remember much about the Crowfoot guy, other than he found some dead body up in the mountains, and he always wore a goofy hat with a bunch of pins on it. If he remembers right, Bernie thinks Crowfoot got fired after a customer complained that he followed her home one night. He'd been hitting on her here earlier while she was having a couple drinks. Creeped her out, I guess. Bernie said she was a typical redhead, hot-tempered, drama queen–type that overreacted to everything."

"Hey, thanks for the information. That helps a lot," Stone said. "Tell Bernie thanks for me too." After the waiter agreed and walked away, Stone looked at me and said, "Hmm, that's interesting."

"Yeah, it is," I agreed. "But a guy hitting on a girl at a bar is not exactly big news, Stone. It certainly doesn't make Rod anything but a typical young guy. Like the waiter said, she may have just been overreacting to Crowfoot's overly flirtatious manner, kind of like the customers at the Food Pantry objecting to Kale's forwardness. Some guys, unfortunately, just don't know how to take 'no' for an answer."

"Yeah, I imagine you're right."

THIRTEEN

Neither Stone nor I was very hungry Saturday evening so we ordered Cobb salads for supper. We decided it was time to pay a visit to Jake Jacoby's house, and if we were going to do that, the best time to catch him at home would be a Sunday, which was tomorrow. We really only wanted to snoop around. We couldn't let Jake know who we were or why we were visiting him. He'd only have to pick up the phone to alert Clay. That made the task more challenging, but certainly not impossible.

I accessed an online phone directory and found a Jake Jacoby listed on Eighth Avenue in Boston. Stone had purchased a map of the city at a service station earlier in the day. We'd booked two rooms at a motel in Boston and packed overnight bags to take along. We were ready to go out-of-state on a sleuthing mission.

We turned in soon after supper and set our alarms to get up early and head for Massachusetts. I sure was getting up early a lot these days, not even to have Ed McMahon standing on the porch with a huge check for me.

We took Stone's car, a red 2003 Z06 Corvette. Four hundred and five horses, zero to sixty in less than four seconds, he told me with pride. I was riding with a Mario Andretti clone. Stone went on to say that this special edition Vette came only with a hardtop. I was more interested in whether it came with antilock brakes, dual airbags, and side impact panels. Despite the alarming rate at which the Corvette was chewing up miles, I managed to doze off halfway to Boston. I was mortified when my own snoring woke me up. I straightened up in my bucket seat and glanced over at Stone. I was relieved to see that he hadn't appeared to notice. He was tapping his fingers lightly on the steering wheel and seemed focused on his driving. I noticed he had very nicely manicured fingernails and wished mine looked as well cared for.

Soon after we'd passed the Boston city limits sign, we stopped at a silk screening shop and had matching shirts printed. Next we stopped to purchase a few items at a law n and garden store. It was early afternoon before we reached Jake's neighborhood.

We pulled into the gas station across from Jake's, and Stone got out of the Corvette. He walked away and then back to the car a minute or two later and handed me a slip of paper.

"You ready for this?" he asked, as I climbed awkwardly over the console into the driver's seat. This proved to be a difficult task in the hard-topped Corvette.

"As ready as I'll ever be," I said, after I'd finally positioned myself behind the steering wheel. I left Stone standing there at the station as I drove his car across the street into Jake's driveway. I parked the Vette next to an older model white Mustang convertible.

I walked up to Jake's door and rang the bell. Then I waited what seemed like a full ten minutes before a good-looking young man opened the door. He was wearing nothing but a pair of sweatpants that were cut off at the knees. I couldn't help but admire his impressive biceps and pectoral muscles. His hair was damp, as if he's just stepped out of the shower. It was a spiked style, brown with blond tips. He had tattoos on both forearms, some sort of dragon tattooed above his left breast, an earring in his right ear, one in his nose, one in his lip, and one through each eyebrow. Didn't those have to have hurt? To me it looked ridiculous on an otherwise handsome guy. It was like wearing your IQ on your face. Why not just take a magic marker and write across your forehead, "I ain't got a lick of sense, and here's holes I had punched in my head to prove it." Maybe it was just another reminder that I'd entered the middle ages.

"Is this 756 Eighth Street?" I asked, trying not to stare at the golden loop earring through his belly button.

"Yes," he answered with a confused look.

"Are you the owner here? Jacoby?" I asked, consulting my notebook, which had a list of fictitious names and addresses written in it. Some of the names had check marks beside them.

"Yes, I'm Jake Jacoby. But I didn't call for an exterminator," he said, pointing at my T-shirt which read Celtic Exterminating on the pocket. I showed no reaction to his comment as I made a check mark next to his name in my notebook.

"No, I know you didn't. A lot of folks in this neighborhood did, however. We've been contracted by the Boston Health Department to spray all the homes in a ten-block area. There's been a recent influx of brown recluse spider bites around here. Two bite victims reported yesterday alone—just up the way." I pointed in the general direction of west, indicating somewhere between next door and the Pacific Ocean. "We sprayed both their houses first thing this morning."

"Oh, I don't know that it's really necessary to—"

"It's required, sir."

"—spray my house."

"Whenever there is a public health epidemic like this one, the health department steps in and takes mandatory steps to eliminate the hazard. As dictated by paragraph two, section five of the department's procedure manual." I was really proud of how competent I sounded.

"There will be no expense levied on any of the residents. In other words, the treatments are free," I explained in simpler terms. After all, I was talking to a guy with a collection of self-induced holes in his head.

"That's good, but still—"

"If you're prepared to—"

"I don't—"

"—vacate the premises for an hour or so, we can get started. I have one of my men getting the sprayer ready. It's out in the trunk."

I noticed Jake look out at his driveway. An odd expression crossed his face when he saw Stone's sports car parked next to his own.

"All of our regular vans are tied up spraying homes, since, of course, the entire neighborhood has been affected," I explained. "Out of necessity, we had to bring Carl's car instead." Don't all exterminators show up in 2003 Corvettes and fill their tiny trunks with sprayers full of toxic chemicals? Jake still looked skeptical, so I had to get more dramatic. I lifted up my pant leg and showed him a large, mottled scar on my calf. A look of revulsion crossed the young man's face as he stared at the disfiguring wound.

"You wouldn't want an ugly scar like this from a bite that takes months to heal," I told him. "Brown recluse bites cause your skin to rot—down to the bone. Very, very painful. You obviously take pride in your body, Mr. Jacoby, treat it as a temple and all. You wouldn't want a bunch of unsightly scars like this all over you, would you? No, I didn't think so. I guarantee you, you wouldn't want to be bitten by a brown recluse."

You wouldn't want to lean up against the hot muffler of your little brother's motorbike either, I thought, as I pulled my pant leg back down over the old burn mark.

"That does look nasty all right," Jake said.

I removed Stone's cell phone from my back pocket and punched in the number written on the slip of paper he'd handed me earlier. "Here, Mr. Jacoby, Leo Friar is on the line. He's the head of the health department." It was a safe bet that a guy Jake's age would have no idea who the director of the local health department was, or even what the department did for the city.

"Hello, Mr. Friar? Uh, this is Jake Jacoby over on Eighth Avenue. I have the Celtic Exterminating people here to spray my house for brown recluse spiders. And—uh—I guess I just wanted to check the situation out," Jake said into the phone. He looked over at me after a few seconds and asked, "What's your name, ma'am?"

"Mandy Hill."

"Yes, Ms. Hill is here. Un-huh, yes, I see. Okay, Mr. Friar. Thanks."

He pushed the "end" button and handed the phone back to me. "I guess it's okay. Mr. Friar said that the stuff you spray is pretty toxic, though. He suggested I find something to do away from the house for an hour or two. I was getting ready to go down to the gym anyway. Could you lock the door when you leave?" Jake asked in a polite manner.

"Of course," I said, and smiled casually. "We always do." I glanced out the window and saw Stone stepping out of the phone booth at the gas station across the street. "My man, Carl, should be right in, and we'll get this one knocked out in a hurry."

Stone came inside a minute or so later, wearing a T-shirt that matched mine and carrying a three-gallon, sloshing, yellow plastic spray bottle. He put on a cheap paper mask that wouldn't keep dust out, much less toxic fumes, and I pulled up an identical one that I had hanging around my neck. Stone started walking around the perimeter of Jake's living room, spraying water into the crevasses where the wall joined the floorboard, just as Jake walked back through the door with a gym bag, his wallet, and car keys.

"Wait a second, Carl. Give Mr. Jacoby a chance to leave so he doesn't breathe in these hazardous fumes. He's getting ready to go to the gym," I said. "Thanks, Mr. Jacoby. Now you'll be able to sleep better at night, knowing that your house is not infested with poisonous spiders. Please leave the front door open when you leave. I'd suggest you give it about an hour and a half, or so, for the fumes to dissipate. Okay?"

"Sure, Ms. Hill. I usually work out for two hours anyway."

"Well, that worked pretty slick, didn't it, Carl. Or is it Leo?" I asked, after Jake had departed.

"It sure did, Ms. Hill."

"How illegal do you reckon this is?" I asked, seriously.

"Well, technically, he did let us in, and he did ask us to lock the door behind us. And, technically, we are spraying his home," Stone said, as he gave the sofa a few squirts of harmless water.

"True. And I'll bet that his home isn't infested with brown recluse spiders tomorrow."

"Assuming it wasn't infested today."

"True again. Well, let's get cracking. You start snooping in the living room and kitchen, and I'll look around in the bedrooms."

FOURTEEN

Jake had the most generic house I've ever been in. It reminded me of a Super Eight Motel room with its lack of personal effects. There were no photos or paintings on the wall, no houseplants or signs of any pets, no knickknacks on shelves, not even a newspaper on the coffee table. Each room held just the basic furniture, and that furniture had a flea market appearance. There was a stereo system in the living room that looked as if it were worth more than everything else in the home put together. Jake had more invested in earrings than he did in home furnishings. Snooping through Jake's place would not take long.

There was one enlarged photo of Jake and another man, walking arm in arm through a heavily wooded area. They were laughing and the sun was glinting off the earrings scattered about Jake's face. The photo was propped up behind the phone on the kitchen counter, as if placed there to remind him to make a call to his friend.

The only other framed photo in the house was on the chest of drawers in Jake's bedroom. It was an eight-by-ten enlargement of Jake with his arm around Clay. Jake was looking at the camera, but Clay looked distracted and disinterested. It was one of those photos that looked like Jake had turned the camera backward, extended his arm as far as he could, and snapped the photo himself. The two men's faces were a bit blurry and distorted. Their eyes looked glazed, as if they were drunk or on drugs.

After I sat the photo back down on the bureau, Stone picked it up again and studied it further. He turned to me and asked, "How's that old saying go—'if you're left, you're right, and if you're right, you're wrong'?"

"I don't know what you're talking about."

"It's an old saying that means that if a man wears an earring in his left ear, he's straight, and if he wears one in his right ear, he's gay."

"Are you saying you think Jake might be gay?"

"It seems highly likely, considering a couple of magazines I found in a drawer in the kitchen." He took me into the kitchen where there was a small desk in the corner. On top of the desk was a roll of stamps, a box of security envelopes, and a pen—bill-paying stuff—and in the desk's only drawer we found bank statements, extra books of checks, two magazines, pens, pencils, a roll of tape, and several packets of developed photos.

Stone removed the magazines. They had the title *Out* across the cover, and one had a photo of two men who reminded me of the one Jake had propped behind his phone.

"Out?" I asked. "Out of what? Out of money? Out of luck? Out of your mind?"

"Out of the closet," Stone answered, dryly.

"Why would Clay live with a gay guy if he's straight?" I asked, my voice rising a notch, as if on the verge of hysteria. This whole situation was getting stranger and stranger. I couldn't imagine what there was about Clay that attracted Wendy so much.

"I don't know," Stone said. "Is it possible he didn't know his roommate was gay, or he just didn't care as long as he had a place to stay during the week? I guess they could have just been friends, and not lovers. I assume gay men have male friends they aren't romantically involved with."

We sorted through the other photos, inside envelopes from a

local one-hour processing store. The outer packets were gone, but the envelopes full of photos and negatives remained. The enlarged photo of Jake and Clay had the original smaller version in one of the packets. There were snapshots of an older couple, possibly Jake's grandparents, several of a golden retriever leaping up to catch a Frisbee, photos of a white-tailed doe and twin fawns, several of bare-chested men lifting weights at the gym, and one of Jake's Mustang convertible with the top down. The only photograph that really grabbed our attention was one of Clay crouched down behind a dead moose. It had been taken at short range; only Clay and the head of the moose were visible in the photo. Over Clay's shoulder in the photo there was a small log cabin that looked to be in a sunny spot deep in the woods. Clay's face was positioned between the two massive antlers of the moose. He was smiling proudly for the camera. There was blood on the hand steadying the right antler and what looked like more blood on the arm of his camouflage shirt.

Stone stared at the photo for a few moments before handing it to me. He pointed to the bottom right corner, "Check this out."

The camera used to take the photo had date-stamp capabilities and in the bottom right corner was a date. "April 12, 2001— Stone, that's the date Eliza disappeared from the Food Pantry parking lot!" I said.

"That would place Clay in the woods on the day his wife was most likely murdered. Could it have been the Adirondacks, near where her body was found? There are increasing numbers of moose there. Or could he have been in a different state?" Stone was thinking out loud, not really expecting an answer from me.

"I would assume that the blood on his hand is from the moose?" I asked.

"Probably so. He would've had to bleed it out," Stone said. For some reason it bothered me that Stone knew so much about hunting, killing, and "bleeding out" moose.

"Do you know what Clay gave as an alibi? Where did he say he was the day Eliza disappeared?" Stone asked.

"According to the newspaper he never did come up with an acceptable alibi for his whereabouts on April twelfth," I said. "Couldn't or wouldn't, I'm not sure which. But the article did say that Clay claimed to be studying alone at a Boston library, although no one could remember seeing him there. The library where I donate my time is much, much smaller. Even then it would be hard for me to recall who all came in there on any given day, so it's not unimaginable that no one could place him there on that date."

"If Clay shot this moose on April twelfth, it was poached, whether he was in New York or Vermont. Moose bear their young in the spring; it can't be legal to shoot moose anywhere that time of year, I wouldn't think. The penalty for poaching is pretty steep, particularly if you are poaching a protected species. Perhaps that's why he didn't want to tell the authorities where he was, or what he was doing, on the day his wife disappeared," Stone said. "I would've thought he'd use that alibi as the lesser of two evils, but then again, he was training at the police academy, and I imagine they frown if their cadets are arrested for any reason."

"Clay wasn't alone, either. Someone else had to have been there to take this photo of him with the dead moose. They're Jake's photos, so I'd say it was obviously Jake. Could Jake have been an accessory to the murder of Clay's wife? If someone like Clay needed assistance in disposing of a wife and unborn child he no longer wanted to be burdened with, whose help would he be more apt to enlist than a guy who was his friend and roommate?" I asked. "But why murder, Stone? Why not divorce?"

"He may have been trying to avoid alimony and child support obligations, or it may have been a 'heat of the moment' type of thing. We also can't rule out the possibility that Clay was not involved in his wife's murder."

I knew Stone was right. I needed to keep an open mind. Clay had constitutional rights and was innocent until proven guilty.

Stone handed me the packets of photos and continued to speak. "Let's take the negatives out of these envelopes, Lexie, and get reprints made. Jake will never miss them. And if he does notice they're gone someday, he'll just think he lost them. By then, he won't even remember us having been here."

I nodded and removed the negatives from the packets. I stuck them inside my notebook. Then I picked up Jake's bank statements, dated just a couple days prior, and glanced at the balances. Jake had $109.26 in his savings account and $31.09 in checking. I hoped for his sake that Monday was payday. I'm glad that I don't have to try and live on a shoestring that short. "What does Jake do for a living?" Stone asked, after I'd shown him the statements.

"I don't know, but inside his checkbook is a pay stub from a place called the Fantasy Club."

Stone picked up a phone directory on the kitchen counter and thumbed through it. After he located the listing for the club, he handed me a pen out of the drawer, and said, "Write this down in your notebook, Lexie."

I wrote the address as he read it to me. Stone waved the phone book and asked, "Should we take this back to Harriet as a souvenir from Massachusetts?"

We put everything back the way we remembered it being when we'd first arrived. We then closed and locked Jake's front door, and headed to the Fantasy Club. Jake wouldn't be there. He'd still be working out at the gym, waiting for the toxic water fumes to dissipate. With any luck at all, we could get a hamburger, a beer, and a few answers at the club, located just nine or ten blocks from Jake's house.

We didn't eat lunch at the Fantasy Club after all. We didn't get a hamburger or even a beer there, but we did eventually get some interesting answers.

Jake Jacoby was a male stripper at an all-male dance club. No wonder he looked so good in just cutoff sweatpants. It was more clothes than he usually wore at work.

After we walked into the dimly lit building, Stone cornered the club's owner, standing behind the bar talking to one of his employees. He flashed a shiny badge, then jammed it back in his rear pocket, and said, "I'm Detective Wesson with the NYPD. Are you Baines McFarland?" He'd gotten the owner's name from the bouncer at the front door. McFarland was a tiny, effeminate-looking man who made Stone look like a Mr. Universe contestant in comparison. Stone dwarfed the club owner, who was about my height, and very slim.

"Yeah, what of it?" Baines replied. He never even glanced at Stone. Instead, Baines turned to his employee, and said, "You can go now, Brett."

Earlier I'd given Stone a photo of my son-in-law taken at Clay and Wendy's wedding. Stone held it up for Baines to see and asked, "Have you seen this individual in your joint?"

Baines glanced at the photo of Clay, gave Stone an insolent look, and then turned away, ignoring him. Stone took another step closer to him and asked, "Do you have a Jake Jacoby working here at your joint?"

"I don't have to answer your questions, copper," Baines finally responded.

"Oh, I think you will."

"This is my club," Baines said, with emphasis on "club," having apparently resented Stone's use of the word "joint" to describe it. "I don't have to answer to you or allow you on my property. So, you and your partner can get your asses out of here right now."

Oh, cool, I thought; now I'm a detective. That's much more fascinating than being an exterminator, or a writer—or, egad, a library assistant. I can't wait to tell my buddies back in Kansas, whom I'm sure will be duly impressed. Or possibly, in the case of a few of my more conservative, stick-in-the-mud-type friends, merely appalled by my acts of subterfuge and deception. Sometimes I wonder how I even acquired such boring pals.

I turned my attention back to the scene unfolding in front of me. Stone was now positioned right in front of Baines McFarland, practically shouting. "My partner, Detective Smith, and I will get our asses out of your sleazy joint just as soon as you answer my questions. You got that, McFarland?"

"You got a search warrant?"

"No, because I hadn't planned on searching the place. I was trying to spare you a lot of grief. But we can play it your way if you'd rather. I can have a search warrant here in ten minutes, along with my team of investigators, who will search this place from top to bottom, looking for any little reason they can find to shut a place like this down. I know it would give them a great deal of pleasure to see this kind of dive become history. They absolutely despise low-class establishments, and gay bars of any kind."

"They won't find anything here illegal, or not within code," Baines challenged.

Stone looked at me, and asked, "What do you think, Detective Smith? Think they'll find a reason to shut this place down?"

"I'd be willing to bet next month's salary that they find a dozen reasons to shut it down," I replied, in my best detective voice.

"Yeah, and you'd win that bet."

Stone turned back to Baines McFarland. "They better not find you've ever served liquor to a minor here, or that you ever do in the future, because your every move will be monitored. And there'd better not be one gram of illegal drugs on the premises or the building will be confiscated. Have you checked your employee's lockers recently? Because if there is one gram, I can guarantee you that my team will find it—while you're down at the station being interrogated on a charge of accessory to murder and/or obstruction of justice." Stone could be very intimidating when he was impersonating an officer. I began to wonder how many crimes we would be guilty of before the day was over. We were on a fairly impressive roll so far.

"I haven't been involved in any murder," Baines countered anxiously, obviously caught off guard by Stone's last remark. "I don't even know what you're talking about."

"So, then what are you trying to hide?"

"Nothing. I'm not trying to hide anything, Wesson. I just don't like cops coming in here threatening me, and demanding answers."

"And I don't like people who aid and abet murderers!"

"I didn't aid or abet anyone!"

"Then do you want to talk to me, or do you want me to go make a call to have a search warrant and the A team here in ten minutes? That's 'A' for asshole, McFarland, because that's what you'll be calling them when they're putting a padlock on your front door."

"All right, all right, Wesson. Jesus, you damn cops are all alike. What the hell do you want to know?" Baines asked wearily.

Stone jabbed the photo of Clay right in the smaller man's face and said, "I want to know if you've ever seen this individual in your 'club', like I asked you before."

This time Baines McFarland studied the photo momentarily, while wiping beads of sweat off his forehead. I noticed a slight tremble in his hand as it held the photo.

"No, never seen him in the club that I recall, but I do know the guy. Can't think of his name right offhand, but he used to live with one of our strippers, Jake Jacoby. He picked Jake up here once when Jake's car was in the shop." He stopped talking as if suddenly afraid he was telling us too much.

"Go on!" Stone said, forcibly.

"I—er—well, I think Jake was kind of sweet on him. I always thought it was odd that this guy lived with Jake. He was training to be a damned cop, like you two. Even had a wife back in New York somewhere, but I heard she got killed a couple years ago."

"That's correct. It was the murder of this guy's wife that Detective Smith and I are investigating. His name's Clay Pitt, by the way. Think there's any chance that Jacoby or Pitt could've been involved in her murder?"

"Well, I didn't know Pitt well enough to speculate about him, but Jake seems like an all right kind of guy. He's got a temper though. And he's built like a brick shithouse too, since he's been spending so much time at the gym. I watched him beat a guy to a bloody pulp here one night, just because the guy flirted with a fellow that Jake had taken a fancy to. He might've killed him if one of my bouncers hadn't pulled him off the poor kid. As it was, the guy lost some teeth and had to have his face stitched back together. I almost fired Jacoby over that. Probably should have."

Stone thanked him for the information. "See how easy that was?" he asked.

Baines, possibly wanting to ensure that Stone had called off the "A" team, said, "Wesson, you might be able to find out more from Bill James. He owns the convenience store down at Twelfth Street and Vine. Jake clerks there for Bill during the day, and works here at night for me."

"Okay, we might just do that. Keep our little conversation to yourself, okay? You wouldn't want to do anything to obstruct justice. I really don't want to have to call my team in, but I will if it becomes necessary. Chances are, Jake's clean anyway."

"No problem, I won't mention it. Frankly, if Jake's involved in murder, I don't want him working here anyway. It's not good for the club's reputation, and I do run a tight ship, Detective Wesson, whether you consider it a sleazy joint or not. I don't like lawsuits. I've already had one filed against me, by the guy Jake pummeled here, the one I was telling you about earlier. It's a hassle that I could do without. I try to avoid any kind of problem, if at all possible."

"I agree with you. It's better to stay within the limits of the law and avoid unpleasant situations, like lawsuits and criminal charges." Stone pulled a pen and small pad of paper out of his pocket and began to write. "Here's my cell phone number if you think of anything else that might help. If you can't reach me there, I'm staying at the Camelot B&B on Union Street in Schenectady while I work on this case. I don't have the number with me, but you can check with directory assistance."

Just the thought of lawsuits and criminal charges had made Baines break out in a sweat again, and he was wiping furiously at his forehead with his sleeve. He nodded, took the information from Stone, and walked away from us to answer a ringing phone. When he picked up the handset, I turned to Stone.

"Detectives Smith and Wesson?" I asked, with a chuckle. "Was that the best you could come up with?"

"Hey, I was ad-libbing, and working under pressure. Fortunately, McFarland was under even more pressure," Stone answered with a sheepish grin.

"And why are you carrying a police badge? Is there something you're not telling me, Stone? Are you really some kind of undercover CIA agent, or does that badge just happen to say 'Captain Courageous' on it?"

"No, I'm not with the CIA, or anything like that—but it is official," Stone said. He smiled at my question. He then removed the shiny metal badge from his pocket for my inspection. "Deputy Officer Stone Van Patten" was inscribed across the badge, under "Myrtle Beach, South Carolina."

"A few years back—right after Diana died—I was bored and restless. I really needed something to do other than working and staring at the walls. I volunteered to be a reserve officer with the local sheriff's office. I still try to put in about ten or twelve hours a week. No pay, but it's been a very interesting and valuable experience. I brought the badge along because I had a hunch it might come in handy."

I laughed at Stone's apparent embarrassment at the admission. "I wish I had your foresight and cleverness, Detective Wesson."

As we left the club, I wondered how a guy with two jobs like Jake Jacoby, who had very few material things, could have less than two hundred dollars in the bank.

Stone entered the little store at Twelfth and Vine to buy us something to drink and also to speak with Bill James if possible. He exited with a couple of Cokes, and an answer to my question about Jake's financial status. Bill was out of town, but unlike Baines McFarland, the clerk behind the counter was more than willing to tell Detective Wesson everything he knew about Jake Jacoby. He had no use for Jake; that much was obvious, Stone said. According to the clerk, our Mr. Jacoby had a boyfriend named Wade, a bad attitude, and an expensive cocaine habit.

FIFTEEN

Stone stepped out onto the back porch on Tuesday morning with a cup of coffee and an amused expression on his face. We'd arrived back at Harriet's on Monday afternoon, after spending the night in Boston and enjoying a wonderful lobster dinner at an outdoor café near a marina. He leaned over the railing of the porch and spat a mouthful of coffee grounds out into the yard, then sat down in his lawn chair.

"Sinbad just called me a birdbrain," he said. "Now why would he call me that when he calls you 'sweetie' most of the time?"

"Must just be a bird with discriminating taste."

"Humph," Stone replied, feigning disgust. "You may have an even meaner streak than Sinbad."

"Well, you know, being called a 'birdbrain' by a parrot might actually be a compliment. And, don't forget, when Sinbad's not calling me 'sweetie' he's referring to me as a 'damn nuisance.' "

"You are kind of a damn nuisance, aren't you 'sweetie'? Lucky for you that you're so damn cute too."

I knew that Stone was joking with me, but I did have to wonder if he wasn't beginning to regret his decision to come to Schenectady to help me. It hadn't been all fun and games, by a long shot.

As if he'd read my mind, he crouched down in front of me. With his free hand under my chin, he tilted my head up so he could look me right in the eyes. I was struck again at how light his blue eyes were.

"Lexie, you do know that I was just teasing, don't you? If I didn't want to be here with you, I wouldn't be. I'm enjoying your company more than I can tell you."

"Good, I'm really enjoying your company too. I feel bad that you had to get involved in this whole convoluted mess, though."

"Don't, Lexie. That's why I came here, remember? To help you through this."

"I was afraid you just wanted to come to determine whether or not you wanted to pursue a relationship with me," I said, somewhat shyly.

"I haven't eliminated that possibility, but it's not the reason I'm here. I've been completely up-front with you. I'd never try to weasel my way into your life. I have more respect for you than that, Lexie. Are you totally opposed to the idea of a relationship with me—sometime in the future, perhaps?"

"No, it's not that at all. I think you're terrific, Stone. I'm just not sure I'm ready to rush into a relationship with anybody right now. But if I did, it would be with you."

"I know you don't want to rush into a relationship. And I certainly don't want to rush you into anything if you're not ready. I'm not a hundred percent sure that I'm ready for a relationship either. But I do know that I find you very attractive, and getting to know you the last few days has made me happier than I've been since I lost my Diana. I think we'll both know if and when we're ready to take the next step, don't you?"

It was the longest speech I'd heard Stone make, and it brought tears to my eyes. I put my hand gently against his cheek, and said simply, "Yes, I do—and thank you. You really are a dear, sweet gentleman."

"Not bad," Stone said, smiling. "From 'birdbrain' to 'dear, sweet gentleman' in less than five minutes."

Harriet soon joined us with her own cup of coffee. When she

sat down on her rusty bucket, we heard more creaking and cracking come out of a one-hundred-pound body than you'd expect to hear out of a ninety-year-old house. It made me think of spraying WD-40 on an old screen door. As she sat down, she let out a sound that resembled air being let out of a tire. It must be dogged determination that kept this old woman going the way she did, not always accomplishing a heck of a lot, but burning off a lot of nervous energy in the process. She was like the embodiment of the Energizer Bunny. Just watching her flitting around the place wore me out.

"Ya going to get on to them chores today, sonny?" Harriet asked Stone.

"Yes, ma'am, right after I finish my coffee," he replied. Then he looked over at my questioning expression, smiled, and said, "I promised Harriet that I'd replace the guts in a couple of her toilet tanks and look at the electrical wiring in the attic for her. She's got a couple of outlets that aren't working properly. I'm kind of a jack of all trades when it comes to home maintenance and general handyman stuff."

"What a nice guy you are, Stone."

"I have my moments, I guess."

"Iffing ya got time, can ya replace a couple boards on the front porch too?" Harriet asked.

Stone chuckled. "Sure, Harriet."

"Reckon ya can take a look-see at my Lincoln too? Made a heap lot of noise the last time I drove 'er. I thinks it were August—maybe."

"You drive a Lincoln?" he asked. I know he was trying to picture this tiny, hundred-pound lady behind the wheel of a block-long vehicle.

"Yep, got one of dem Continentals. Bought 'er new in seventy-eight. The feller there at the car store told me to bring 'er in fer an earl change when I got three thousand miles on 'er.'"

"You mean he told you to have the oil changed every three thousand miles?"

"No, he said 'when you get 'er up to three—' "

Stone cut in. "Harriet, do you mean you've just now put three thousand miles on your twenty-five-year-old car?"

"Well, not quite, but it's getting close to that many. Food store's only a few blocks down, and I walks there unless I gots to git lots of stuff."

"So this is the first time you've put new oil in it, in the twenty-five years you've owned it?"

"Yep, just doing like the feller said. Hell, the gas in 'er was put in about ninety-nine, I'd reckon. Getting perty good mile-age in 'er, iffing ya ask me."

"Hmm, okay," Stone said, wide-eyed. "Maybe I should give the old girl a thorough check-up. Only putting a few miles a year on a car can be tough on them. The oil should be changed a couple of times a year, at the very least, no matter how many miles are put on the engine. It may take a jackhammer to get the old oil out of her. And the gas can turn to shellac if it sits in a tank that long."

"Yeah, well—whatever, sonny. Still runs good, so just give 'er a look-see when you gits time."

"Okay, no problem," Stone said. "I'll look the Lincoln over real good for you. I just can't imagine a 1978 Continental with less than three thousand miles on it."

"Well, it were a 'demo,' or that's what that car store feller called it. Damn fool joyriding salesman had already put eleven or twelve hunderd on it 'fore I got it."

Stone just shook his head slowly back and forth, with his chin cupped in his hand. "Tell you what, Harriet. Why don't you make me a list of everything you need fixed, replaced, or inspected, and I'll work my way through it as I have time."

"All righty, and maybe I could give ya a break on yer rent," she offered, hesitantly.

"No, I wouldn't think of charging you, Harriet. I enjoy doing that kind of thing and it is really no bother at all. I'll let you pay for any parts or materials needed, but I'll donate the labor. Sound fair enough?"

"Shore, sonny," Harriet said, and flashed him a broad, toothy smile. From years of smoking unfiltered Pall Malls, Harriet's teeth were the color of tobacco. I wondered if they were false. I'd have bet that she still had her own teeth, because I couldn't imagine Harriet would ever submit to false teeth. I also wondered how long it'd been since Stone had been called "sonny." Then Harriet turned to me and asked, "How's it going on that there Pitt case?"

We'd let Harriet think that Stone and I were friends from way back and that he'd been employed to help me with my research for the freelance article I was writing. Why start telling anybody the truth now? "Going pretty well, so far. It's been a big help having Stone here to assist me. We've been able to gather quite a bit of information. Working together these last few days has been very beneficial."

"Otter go talk to that boy's mudder, iffing ya get a chance," Harriet said.

"Clayton Pitt's mother?"

"Yep. 'Nitwit Pitt' I calls her."

"Does she live around here?" I asked. Nitwit Pitt? Oh my. "Where's his father?"

"She shore does live 'round here. Nuttier than a fruitcake, his mudder is. Don't rightly know what e'er become of his pappy, though."

"Where does Mrs. Pitt live, Harriet?"

"Oh, 'bout ten miles south of here, where they lock up all

115

dem nutcases. Don't know what the place is called, but it's out offa I-90 somewheres."

Stone utilized Harriet's phone books again, and after a few calls, found a Wanda Pitt registered at a home for the "mentally challenged," called Serenity Village. As Harriet had indicated, it was about ten miles south, right off I-90. It was a state-operated, assisted-living facility, with round-the-clock nursing and psychological therapy.

After much discussion, we decided it would be best if I went to see Wanda Pitt alone. It would be a good opportunity for Stone to tackle the list of chores that Harriet had drawn up for him. His to-do list included everything from "sevin dust punkin" to "fix crappers." Harriet knew a good thing when she saw it, and she was going to take full advantage of Stone's handyman abilities.

Stone had already inspected and serviced the Lincoln. He said that there was a dent or ding on every corner of the vehicle. "Harriet must bang into something every time she drives it up the street to the store," Stone had said, laughter in his voice. "She uses that car as if it were a battering ram, instead of a mode of transportation. Remind me not to park my Corvette anywhere near the garage or driveway."

Sixteen

With Stone and Harriet's directions, I had no problem finding Serenity Village. I told the lady at the front desk that I was Clara Pitt, Wanda's niece. She pointed the way down the hall, back to Wanda's private two-room apartment.

I knocked and waited for Wanda to open the door. I was shocked by the appearance of Wendy's mother-in-law. Wanda was a huge woman, no less than four hundred pounds. I felt absolutely anorexic standing next to her. She had several teeth missing, and the few that remained were rotting. She looked, tragically, as if she maintained a steady diet of fat and refined sugar. Her hair had not seen a comb or brush in days, I was sure, and no shampoo for even longer.

"Mrs. Pitt?" I asked, pleasantly, trying to mask my repulsion.

"Yeah?"

"Hi, how are you? I'm Clara Ransfield, from Serenity Village's administrative office. I'm here to see if there's anything you need, and to update our files." I waved the notebook I was carrying as if it were full of official files and data. "May I come in and talk with you for a few minutes?"

"Guess so," she said, and stepped back to allow me to enter her apartment. I walked over to a couch along the back wall of her living room and sat down. She plopped down in an oversized recliner across from me. "What did you say you're name was?" she asked.

"Clara Ransfield. Please call me Clara."

"Okay, I'll call you Clara," she said, nodding, and causing her numerous chins to ripple like the wind blowing across a wheat field. "Put chocolate on your list, Clara. I need chocolate. My candy keeps getting stolen, and these people here know that without it I get severe headaches. Pepsi too. They haven't brought me any Pepsi in days. They ought to be more considerate than that, don't you think? To let a person suffer like this and all—well, it just ain't right. Guess I should expect it, since they all hate me and have been trying to make me miserable for all the years I've been here. It ain't nothing new."

I wrote "Pepsi" and "Chocolate" in my notebook, underneath "Obese" and "Neurotic." "I'll see that you get what you need, Mrs. Pitt."

"About time somebody did." Wanda reached over and flicked off her television. She had been watching a popular daytime soap.

"How long have you been a resident here at Serenity Village?" I had feared she'd be reluctant to give me any personal information, but it didn't take long to begin getting interesting and sensational details out of Clay's mother.

"Around sixteen years, I reckon. Ever since I killed my husband, anyway."

"Excuse me?" I nearly fainted at her nonchalant response.

"Homer was a drinker, and when he drank, he became abusive. He put me in the hospital more times than I can remember. But he came at me one too many times, missy. The last time he attacked me, I grabbed a butcher knife out of the dishwasher to protect myself, and the damn fool ran right into it. I'd had enough of the bastard's abuse anyway. Homer bled to death on the kitchen floor. I made sure he was beyond saving before I called the police. My boy, Clayton, was there too—seen the whole thing. He testified in court for me that I killed his father in self-defense. Clayton despised his old man, and with little wonder." Wanda was much more articulate than I would have guessed she'd be from my first impression of her. For a woman who'd been through what she had, I felt she spoke fairly intelligently.

"How horrible for you and your son. How old was your boy at the time?" I didn't want to let on that I'd ever even heard of Clay.

"Fourteen, maybe fifteen. Been on his own since then. They put me in this home for whackos, and they haven't let me go home since. The sons-a-bitches, anyway."

"So, your husband had a long history of abusing you?"

"Oh, yeah, that's the understatement of the year. Homer was mean and sadistic—the kind of loser my mother warned me about. Beat on Clayton even more than he beat on me—and that's saying a lot. Used to use Clayton as a punching bag. Put cigarettes out on his legs, then called him a sissy and a crybaby when he squalled. I had to kill Homer to protect my son, if for no other reason. But I had plenty of reasons, let me tell you."

"How has all that affected your son, seeing his father killed and all? It must have been really traumatizing for a young boy that age. What kind of person is Clayton now?"

"Can't tell you. I ain't seen that boy in . . . well, probably ten years. But when he was young he was sure an ornery kid. Used to pick up pop bottles off the road and turn them into a nearby store for the refunds. He saved his bottle money and bought a pellet gun when he was about twelve. Used to bring home rabbits, squirrels, and even a cat now and then, which he'd shot while he was out hunting. He even got thrown into a home for juvenile delinquents for a spell, right after he broke into his school and slashed the throats of several animals in the school lab—a guinea pig, some hamsters, and a few mice. He had a bit of his daddy in him. But then, what could you expect? He was always good to the puppy he'd rescued, though. I'll give him credit for that much. Clayton had found him abandoned in an alley and named him Buddy. Still had him last I knew, but he'd be pretty old by now. I hope Clayton's outgrown some of that meanness. I wouldn't want him to grow up and be good-for-nothing like his father. But I never hear from him anymore, so I couldn't really tell you what he's like now."

"Do you know why he doesn't come around to visit anymore?" I asked.

"Don't know. People around here probably told him I was crazy and poisoned his mind against me. Gets kind of lonely, because no one around here speaks to me much. My birthday is in a few days. Clayton used to always visit me on my birthday, but he hasn't in years. I bet I won't see another living soul on my birthday this year. You're the first person to visit me in a long, long time. What'd you say your name was again?"

"Clara," I said. I felt sorry for this poor woman who had married an evil, cruel man, and spawned a carbon-copy son with him. It was easy to understand why she sat in her little apartment, watching soap operas and eating herself to death.

"Wanda, I appreciate your time. Is there anything else you need?"

"Maybe a book or two. I like to read them Harlequins once in awhile."

"I'll see to it that you get some of them." Talking to Wanda made me want to cry. The poor woman had led such a horrific life. She was now living vicariously through soap operas and romance novels, probably visualizing herself living a kind of fairy-tale life she had never, and would never, personally experience.

"One last thing before I have to leave, Wanda," I said. "Do you know if your son, Clayton, has ever married? He is your only child, isn't he?"

"Yeah, Homer threw such a fuss when I got pregnant with

Clayton that I never dared get knocked up again. Anyway, Clayton married a gal named Elizabeth, or something like that. Was told she had bright red hair, like Homer's. But that's the last I heard. I can't even recall who told me that," Wanda said, obviously trying to think back to recall who had given her the information. Finally, she shook her head and shrugged. "That's all I know. Carol, wasn't it?"

Close enough. I nodded as I got up off the couch and got ready to leave. I patted Wanda gently on the shoulder, and said, "Well, I'll let you get back to your television program, Wanda. I'll see that you get the items you've told me you needed."

"Thanks, and thanks for visiting me too," Wanda said. "Be careful now, as you're leaving. There are little purple creatures from Jupiter that live in the hallways and stairwells here. They've got only one eye in the middle of their foreheads. They have furry feet, and great big teeth. I think they're the little sons-a-bitches that keep stealing all my candy."

Harriet's words came back to me: "Nuttier than a fruitcake, his mudder is." With a nod and a tender smile, I tried to mask the veil of sorrow that had suddenly dropped over me.

Before driving back to the Camelot B&B, I stopped by the drugstore and picked up a few items. On my way back past Serenity Village, I dropped a bag off at the front desk and asked the young gal sitting there to deliver it to Wanda Pitt. She promised she would take it to Wanda right away. The bag contained a half dozen Harlequin romance books, the latest edition of Soap Opera Digest, two six-packs of Pepsi, and two five-pound boxes of chocolate candies.

I vowed to myself to send a few books and a box of chocolates to Wanda every month or so. It would give her something to look forward to. She needed something, no matter how trivial, to look forward to in her sad and lonely life. With any luck at all, Wanda could eat at least a few of the chocolates before the purple, one-eyed, furry-footed, aliens stole them from her.

SEVENTEEN

The smell of bacon woke me on Wednesday morning. I got dressed, brushed my teeth, and spent a few minutes fussing with my hair. When I went downstairs and walked into the kitchen, three voices in unison greeted me. "Good morning, sweetie." Then Sinbad tacked on an, "Ya damn nuisance," in a perfect imitation of his master.

Stone was sitting at the table. In front of him was a plate full of bacon, French toast, and scrambled eggs. It looked and smelled delicious, and I found myself suddenly extremely hungry. Now this is what I'd had in mind from the beginning!

"Would ya like some breakfast this morning?" Harriet asked me.

"Yes, ma'am, I would love breakfast this morning," I answered with feeling. My mouth was watering in anticipation as I gazed at Stone's plate. "That looks wonderful. It smelled so good it actually woke me up."

I saw Harriet glance up at the clock above the stove. It read seven-thirty-five. I knew she was thinking half the day was already wasted. She shook her head in amazement and then opened the fridge door and removed a carton of eggs. As she turned back toward the stove, I noticed there was a full inch of ash hanging precariously off the end of her cigarette over the skillet. I decided to concentrate on the antics of the parrot to preserve my appetite.

"How'd you get a breakfast like that? And at this time of

day?" I whispered to Stone as I gestured toward his meal.

"Oh, probably because I'm such a handsome, charming fellow," he said. "And fixing Harriet's toilets for her probably helped too."

"Suck-up," I whispered back good-naturedly.

I decided that Harriet might have better hearing than I thought when she said, "Stone says his favorites be French toast and bacon. But don't worry, sweetie, I knows what ya likes too."

With that remark, she placed a full platter of poached eggs and toast down in front of me. I looked down at my plate and back up at Stone just in time to see him laugh hard enough to spit a piece of bacon the full length of the table.

"Thank you, Harriet. This looks delicious," I said politely as I kicked Stone's shin. My appetite had vanished, much like Eliza Pitt had vanished on that April morning two and a half years prior. My fork felt as if it weighed twenty pounds as I picked it up off the table.

"Chow down, sweetie. Times a'wasting!"

Later on that evening, Stone got a phone call from his favorite nephew, Andrew. Andy was a pilot, Stone said. He flew private charters out of a small, executive airport, not far from Stone's home. He was going to be flying into New York the following Monday to drop off some clients. After a few days, he would fly the same clients back to South Carolina. Andy had decided to rent a car and stay in New York until the scheduled return flight, in order to spend some time with his uncle. Harriet had several vacancies, and Stone arranged for Andy to use one of the available rooms.

"You'll love Andy," Stone told me. "He's a terrific young man. I wish I could have made a jeweler out of him, but he's always wanted to fly, from the time he was just a little boy. My brother Sterling is Andy's dad, and he's a commercial pilot for

Continental Airlines. But Andy never wanted to fly the huge jetliners like Sterling. I guess I should be thankful that Andy chose to settle near me in Myrtle Beach."

"I can't wait to meet Andy," I said. And I meant it sincerely. Anybody who rated so highly with a man like Stone had to be a wonderful individual.

Stone and I watched the evening news together on a little thirteen-inch color television in Harriet's family room, before retiring to our own rooms. We were riveted to the screen when a blurb came on about a new breakthrough in the 2001 Eliza Pitt murder case.

Apparently, the Schenectady homicide detective, Ron Glick, had recently reopened the investigation, in association with the DeKalb police department. It thrilled me to think that perhaps I'd had a stronger influence on the detective than I'd realized.

According to the news release, Kale Miller, the boy who had bagged Eliza's groceries at the Food Pantry on the day she vanished, had remembered that she'd been wearing a gray sweatshirt with Mickey Mouse on the front. Deep in the Adirondack Mountains, a sweatshirt matching that description had been found approximately three miles from where the hiker, Rod Crowfoot, had discovered the body two weeks after Eliza's disappearance.

The camera zoomed in on Detective Glick's face, making it appear even squarer than I recalled. It seemed to be the exact same shape as the TV screen. Glick explained to the reporter how DNA tests had determined that the blood on the sweatshirt, and also the blood splattered on a nearby rock, matched the blood of Eliza Pitt. It was thus concluded that her body had been discovered in a different location from the site where the murder had actually taken place.

"It was a brutal killing," Detective Glick said into the camera. "The victim died from a blow to the skull with a blunt object, presumably a rock."

The television screen showed a photo of a pregnant Eliza Pitt, taken before the murder, on the TV screen. It was the first photo I'd seen of her in color. The only other photo had been a black and white, grainy photo in an April 2001 edition of Schenectady's *Daily Gazette*. Like the girl at the Starlight Lounge that Rod Crowfoot had followed home one night, and also like Clay's father, Homer, Eliza Pitt had bright red hair. Wanda Pitt had at least been correct on that account.

When I checked my e-mail Thursday morning, a message I received from Wendy about caused me to go into cardiac arrest.

"Mom," she wrote, "I've got terrible news. Something really bad has happened. Please call me as soon as you can. I need you—when are you coming home?"

I considered abandoning my Jeep and catching the next flight back to Kansas City. I knew that it was an overreaction to all that had been going on recently. So I forced myself to calm down and then rushed out to look for Stone.

I found him in the backyard, digging a hole for Harriet, who was standing beside him with a sweet potato vine growing out of a pint Mason jar. I had noticed the sweet potato propped up in the glass jar, full of roots, with vines stretched out all along the window ledge behind the kitchen sink. I'd known there was something vital missing from the backyard; I just hadn't been able to put my finger on it.

As Harriet bent down to place the sweet potato and its roots down into the freshly dug hole, Stone sensed my presence and turned to gaze at me on the porch. He was at my side in an instant.

"What's wrong, Lexie?" he asked.

I repeated the message I'd received from Wendy as best I could, my voice quivering as I spoke. Stone pulled me into an embrace and patted my back tenderly as he said, "Go get my cell phone off my bureau and call her right away. Maybe it's not as bad as you're anticipating. And remember that I'm here for you. Okay?"

EIGHTEEN

Wendy had lost the baby. She said she'd awakened the previous night with terrible stomach cramps and Clay had driven her to the ER at Shawnee Mission Medical Center. It'd been an ectopic pregnancy. My grandchild never had a chance for survival.

Wendy was distraught and heartbroken. I was upset for her, knowing how much the baby meant to her. But here was another example of how God sometimes works in mysterious ways, I thought. Had the baby lived, Wendy would be forever tied to a man who might one day be tried and convicted of murder. The child would also have a tough time of it, with a felon for a father. If tried and convicted, it was possible that Clay could even receive the death penalty.

As I listened to Wendy talk about Clay's reaction, or lack of one, to the loss of their child, I knew she was upset with his attitude. Clay wasn't offering the support and compassion she needed. It seemed to me he was emotionally distancing himself from her when she needed him the most. It seemed as though Clay thought the tragedy wasn't worth getting upset about, and he didn't want to discuss the loss or be emotionally disturbed by it.

"I wish you were here with me, Mom," Wendy said in a teary voice as we spoke on the telephone.

"Honey, how soon do you have to start your new job at the coroner's office?"

"Not for several weeks now, because of the time required for my recovery from the surgery to remove the fetus and placenta from my fallopian tube. Why do you ask?"

"I'd like you to consider flying out here to spend a week with me. You need to get away to cope with the loss of your baby, and I really need to discuss something with you." I wanted to take this opportunity to warn her about Clay while she was upset with him. Now she might be more open to the idea that she didn't know him as well as she thought she did. I could only pray for that possibility.

"What do you need to discuss with me?" she asked, suspicion evident in her voice.

"It's not something I want to talk with you about on the phone."

"Oh God, Mom! You're not moving to Myrtle Beach to live with that Stone guy, are you?"

"No, of course not, Wendy. It has nothing to do with him, or me, for that matter. But it's critically important to you and your future."

"Mom, what in the world are you talking about? You're scaring me."

"I'm sorry, honey. I don't mean to scare you. But I do really, really need you out here—just for a week if that's all you can get away."

"Well, it does sounds tempting, but I'm not sure what Clay will think about me leaving him for a week this early in our marriage."

"If he's any kind of husband at all, he'll understand you need to deal with this tragedy in your own way. Unless he's a total jerk, he won't prevent you from doing whatever you have to do to recover."

I knew I was being melodramatic, but I'd hoped she'd consider coming, if for no other reason than to prove to her mother that she hadn't married a total jerk.

"And honey, it wouldn't be wise to tell him I have something important to discuss with you. No sense worrying him. Just tell him you need to get away, or your mother needs you—and that your mother is paying your way. Tell him anything you have to, but please let me arrange for a plane ticket for you to come out here."

I'd just encouraged my daughter to lie. But I knew I had to keep my priorities straight. And my daughter's safety was at the top of the list at the moment.

"I'll talk to Clay when he gets home from the gym," Wendy assured me. "I'll call you back at this same number after I've discussed it with him."

"Okay, I'll be waiting to hear from you. And I'm so sorry to hear about your baby. There will be others, but I know that doesn't make it any easier to accept."

I gave her the number to Stone's cell phone. She wouldn't have to wonder about that aspect of it anyway. Stone's phone had a South Carolina preface. Stone borrowed a deck of cards from Harriet and talked me into a game of rummy. I assumed it was designed to take my mind off the ticking clock. He suggested the three of us could drive up through Maine and New Hampshire. If Wendy didn't take me up on my offer, just he and I could go, he said.

"That's where the fall colors are the most vivid. It'd be a relaxing place for Wendy to recover from her loss. I'd treat you both to a Maine lobster while we were there. By the way, Lexie, how do you plan to relay all of this information to Wendy?"

"I don't know. I'll need to be tactful, of course. I've never cared for Clay much, but Wendy loves him. I know it won't be an easy thing to do. Couldn't I just make small talk with Wendy and casually work it into the conversation?"

"How would you do that?"

"Maybe something like, 'It sure is cool today, isn't it,

Wendy'?" I ad-libbed. "I hear we're to have a bit of rain this weekend. Would you like to go with me to the weekend sale at Sears? Someone told me that Rose Travis got hired at the hair salon at Sears. There's a high probability that your husband is a cold-blooded killer. Did you notice how well the yellow rose bushes in the front yard are doing since I pruned them? Maybe I'll have Rose give me a perm this weekend while I'm at the sale at Sears."

Stone shook his head and laughed at my preposterous rendition. I was being silly, but Stone and I both knew it really wasn't a laughing matter. Stone knew me well enough by now to know I often laughed to keep from crying. As a lone tear escaped my eye and trailed down my cheek, he put his arm around me to comfort me. "It will work out, honey," he said softly. "Try to think positive thoughts."

I prayed silently that he was correct and it all would work out—and in a way that didn't alienate my daughter. I also prayed Wendy would make the trip out East, and that she'd like Stone and accept him as my new friend. For I realized I was beginning to care a lot for Stone Van Patten, and I was still not too sure I was ready for that kind of complication in my life.

At long last, Stone's cell phone rang. Wendy said she was coming! I was so relieved I almost wept. Clay had not been receptive to the idea but had finally agreed to the trip. I told her I would arrange for a paperless ticket. All she'd have to do was show her identification at the ticket desk at KCI Airport in Kansas City, Missouri. It was late Thursday evening, so I'd try to schedule a flight for Monday morning to give her several days to rest and recuperate from her surgery.

I handed Stone's phone back to him, and then in an impulsive gesture I reached up and placed a quick kiss on the side of his cheek. With a thoughtful look, he said, "Don't worry. Everything is going to work out just fine, Lexie. We'll make sure Wendy is safe. Get your ticket bought—I'll be on the back porch reading for another hour or so. If you need to make any calls, my phone will be on the bureau in my room. Every month I waste more airtime minutes than I use, so feel free to use it all you want."

Earlier that day, we had picked up the reprints we'd ordered from Jake's negatives. Stone had requested enlargements of the photo of Clay with the dead moose on April twelfth, and the one of Jake and Clay together. In the larger version of the moose photo, we could just make out an unusual etching of an eagle on the front door, as if the carved wooden door had been specially made for the cabin. The only other interesting thing we learned from the photo was that there was a high-powered rifle propped up against the head of the moose, between its left antler and Clay. Stone thought it was probably a thirty-aught-six, often used for hunting big game. "You know, Lexie, Clay didn't kill that moose with his bare hands," Stone reminded me. "Or thump it over the head with a rock."

NINETEEN

Wendy's flight was scheduled to leave KCI airport at ten-fifteen Monday morning. She'd change planes in Atlanta and arrive at JFK in New York just after four in the afternoon. At nine o'clock Kansas City time, ten o'clock eastern, Stone's cell phone rang, startling us both.

We were in a small café, halfway to JFK Airport, having English muffins, coffee, and a light-hearted conversation about the unusual reasons we'd had to visit the hospital emergency room when we were kids. Stone had gotten his tongue stuck to a freezer door at the grocery store one day, and another time he'd broken an ankle jumping off the roof of his house, using a beach towel as a cape. I had super glued my lips together by trying to remove the lid of the tube with my teeth, and once I had shoved a kernel of corn up my nose just to see if it'd fit. It did, but then it wouldn't come back out on its own. We laughed at ourselves, and at one another's childhood mishaps.

We were lingering over breakfast because there was time to pass. We'd left Schenectady in the wee hours of the morning in order to allow extra time to negotiate the traffic between Schenectady and New York City. We'd brought my Jeep since Stone's Corvette was a two-seater, and we'd have three people and Wendy's luggage on our trip back to Schenectady. Stone understood I wanted to arrive early rather than risk Wendy exiting the plane and finding no one waiting for her.

Stone's nephew Andy would be registered into his room at

the Camelot B&B by the time we arrived with Wendy. I had booked the last of the four bedrooms on the second floor for her. She would share my bathroom, and Stone and Andy would share the other upstairs bathroom. Andy was only five years older than Wendy, so Stone and I hoped they'd have a lot in common. It might also make it easier for her to accept my relationship with Stone, which at this point was strictly platonic. I hoped for my daughter's approval before I opted for a more personal relationship with Stone.

When Stone answered his phone and handed it to me, I feared that Wendy had changed her mind about making the trip East. "Who answered your phone, Mom?" Wendy asked. "That Stone guy? Are you with him now?"

"Yes, Wendy, that was Stone. It's Mr. Van Patten's phone number you called. Where are you, honey?" I asked, changing the subject as quickly as possible.

"I'm at the Kansas City International Airport. I just got my flight information, and I think they've screwed up and booked me onto the wrong flight."

"What do you mean?"

"They've listed my destination as JFK in New York."

"Well, actually that's the way I booked it."

"Why? I thought you were in Myrtle Beach. I thought I'd be flying into Charleston. Clay brought me to the airport, and he's really upset and concerned that my plane is going to New York, and not South Carolina."

"No reason for him to be concerned. Right after your arrival, Stone is taking us to Maine and New Hampshire. That's where the fall colors are the most vivid, and since New York is on the way, it just made sense to pick you up there."

"I don't know about this, Mom. I don't think I should go out there. Clay's all stirred up, and I'm not sure I'm up to meeting your new boyfriend right now. You know, you should have told me he'd be with you."

"Wendy, listen to me. I couldn't tell you that at the time," I said sternly, talking to her as if she were thirteen again. "Whether or not Stone is my boyfriend is irrelevant at the moment. And I don't give a damn how stirred up Clay is right now. I want you on that plane at ten-fifteen. Do you understand me?"

"Or what? Are you going to ground me? Geez, Mom! Why are you acting this way? What's going on?" Wendy was losing her composure as fast as I was. I knew she thought I was hanging on to my sanity by a very thin thread.

I tried to sound calm so she wouldn't get any more upset. "Is Clay there beside you right now?"

"No, he went to get us some coffee to drink while we're waiting for my boarding time. But now I'm thinking maybe we should just turn around and go back home."

"No! You cannot go back home, Wendy! I mean it! Dammit, listen to me for once."

"Why? Why, Mom? Why are you doing this to me?"

"Honey, I'm not trying to do anything to you," I said with a sigh. I hadn't wanted to tell her about her husband this way, but I had run out of options. "I'm trying to keep Clay from doing something to you. That's what I'm trying to do!"

"What?" Wendy yelled into the phone. "What are you talking about?"

"Wendy, listen to me. There are things you don't know about Clay's past that you need to know to protect yourself. He's not the guy he appears to be. Trust me."

"You've got to be kidding, Mom. Is that Stone guy putting you up to this?"

"Stone has nothing to do with this—whatsoever." I glanced up at Stone with a look of apology. He smiled reassuringly and nodded. He was letting me know that I was taking the right approach. I had to get my daughter on that plane, even if it took scare tactics to do it. But I really didn't know how much to tell her at this point. I didn't want to scare her, or upset her, at least not to the point where she wouldn't behave in a normal way around Clay when he came back with the coffee. But I had to scare her enough to make sure she got on her scheduled flight. "Wendy, did you know that you're Clay's second wife? Are you aware that Clay has been married before?"

"He has not!"

"He has, Wendy. I have proof of it. When his first wife was six months pregnant with his child, she disappeared and was found by a hiker a couple of weeks later. She'd been murdered in the Adirondack Mountains, beat to death with a rock. Clay is a suspect in her murder."

Wendy gasped over the phone. "Huh? What do you mean? Clay went to a cabin in those mountains all the time. To kill moose, Mom, not pregnant women."

"Yes, he bagged his moose illegally too, but that's the least of our concerns right now. Does the log cabin Clay stayed in have an eagle etched in the door?"

Wendy gasped again. She began to whisper, "Yes. Oh, geez—oh my goodness. How did you know that? He took me there once and it—oh my—no, no, Mom. It must be all a mistake. Clay would have told me. Wouldn't he, Mom? Wouldn't he tell me something as important as that? A murdered wife and child, for goodness sake!" She sounded as if she were going into shock, becoming hysterical. She didn't want to believe what I was telling her. I can't say I blamed her.

Memories of Wendy as a child flashed through my mind. She'd be shaking her head violently, her eyes squeezed shut, and her hands over her ears, when she was being told something she didn't want to hear. I could picture her standing in the airport doing the exact same thing right now. At least she was

beginning to believe I knew too much for it all to be coinciden-
tal. She surely knew by now there had to be at least a grain of
truth to all I'd told her. She also knew I'd never invent a story
just to hurt her. I'd hurt myself before I'd intentionally hurt
her.

"Apparently he didn't tell you about any of it, honey. Do you
happen to know his old roommate in Boston?"

"Jake?"

"Yes, Jake Jacoby."

"Uh-huh. Clay moved in with Jake shortly before Clay and I
started dating. Clay told me he'd met Jake after Jake joined the
same gym. Jake is the guy who owns the little cabin in the
mountains. He inherited it from an uncle, I think Clay said."

"Wendy, did Clay ever tell you his roommate, Jake Jacoby,
was gay, or that he's a cocaine addict?"

"Jesus, Mom! How do you know all this?"

"Stone's been helping me investigate the situation. We've
found out a lot of things you should know. Enough that we're
concerned for your safety in regards to Clay."

"Oh, Lord—do you think Clay would hurt me? You do, don't
you? Why does all this have to happen now? You know, I
wondered sometimes if Jake was gay—"

"He's a stripper."

"At some club."

"At an all men's club, Wendy."

"Oh, geez. No kidding? Well, Jake hated me, Mom. I can tell
you that much, anyway. He tried everything he could to get
Clay to break up with me. He didn't want Clay to have anything
to do with me, almost as if he was jealous of our relationship. I
knew Jake did coke occasionally. He even turned Clay on to it.
But Clay knows I'm against drugs of any kind, and he swears
he's not doing any now. I found some in the glove compartment
of his truck the other day, but he told me it wasn't his."

"Honey, think about that for a minute. How often do people put expensive, illegal drugs in someone else's glove compartment and then forget about them? Not too often, wouldn't you say? That's just an excuse, a cop-out."

"Yeah, I know," Wendy said, with resignation in her voice. "I knew in my mind the drugs belonged to Clay. But my heart didn't want to believe it. I was in denial, I guess. I wanted to ignore the evidence in hopes it'd go away."

Wendy had fallen silent. I could hear her breathing hard over the phone, almost hyperventilating. I tried to comfort her, tried to calm her down as much as I could and assure her everything would work itself out. "Everything will be okay, Wendy. Don't worry, honey. Stone and I, and Andy—Stone's thirty-two-year-old nephew—will take care of everything. Among the four of us we'll get things worked out. I don't want you to be concerned about anything but getting on the plane, Wendy."

My right hand was on the table next to my coffee cup. It had begun to tremble as if afflicted with a temporary palsy. Stone reached over and clasped my hand in his. He was trying to calm me, as I was trying to calm Wendy.

"I can't believe all this, Mom." Then her whispering grew even fainter, and she sounded panicky. "You know, Mom, I didn't want to tell you this, but Clay's whole personality seemed to change when he found out I was expecting a baby. He became almost hostile to me, as if I'd done something wrong, something intentionally designed to hurt him. He acted as if I'd betrayed him. I still can't understand why he reacted the way he did to my pregnancy. But when I lost the baby, he seemed almost relieved—like a tremendous burden had been lifted from his shoulders."

"Do you know what Clay's childhood was like?" I asked. "Has he ever talked to you about it? From what I found while talking to his mother, Wanda—if you can believe her, anyway—

his childhood was pretty grim. Clay's father was an alcoholic and a child and spouse abuser. His mother is in a home for the mentally ill. Wanda said she'd been there for around sixteen years."

"You talked to Clay's mother?" Wendy asked, incredulously. "I knew Wanda was alive, and his father, Homer, was mean. Clay said his mother was unable to come to the wedding because of health problems, but he never said she was mentally ill. He didn't mention his father at all, remember? Clay never said much about his family, though, other than he was an only child like me. He left home when he was about fifteen and joined the Navy soon after."

Wendy's voice dropped even lower. I could hardly make out her next words. "Here comes Clay, Mom. I see him walking this way. I don't know what to do—oh, Lord—what do I do? What do I do, Mom?"

"Listen to me, Wendy, and do exactly as I tell you. Behave as normally as you possibly can. Tell Clay you talked to me and we're all heading up to Maine and New Hampshire from here, so I thought it'd make sense to have you fly into JFK instead of Charleston. Don't mention anything about the rest of this. Okay? Promise me that, Wendy. Not one word that anybody suspects him of anything. Promise!"

"I promise," she whispered. She sounded a little calmer, but I still worried she wouldn't be able to pull it off in front of her new husband. "What if he doesn't believe me, Mom? You know I never was a good liar. Oh gosh, I've got to go. He's almost here now. He's almost here. I heard him on his cell phone. I think he's talking to Jake. I heard him say Jake's name. Jake still calls him every day. What do I do? Oh, God, what do I do?"

"Stay calm. Don't say anything to Clay about anything. Just get on the plane. Whatever happens, Wendy, just get on that plane! We'll take care of you once you get here. Not a word to

Clay about anything now, you hear me? Tell him he doesn't need to stay with you while you wait to board the plane. Tell him he can go back to the house—that you'll be fine waiting there by yourself." I was whispering into the phone now. I tried to reinforce the things she'd need to do, and keep her calm at the same time. "We'll see you in a just a few hours. Okay, honey? Act normal now, okay? I love you."

"Me too," she said. And then the phone went dead and I collapsed in nervous tears.

TWENTY

The engine sputtered as Stone guided my Jeep Wrangler to the shoulder of the road. The vehicle took one final gasp and died. It rolled to a stop along the busy interstate. I noticed in alarm that steam was pouring out from under the hood.

"Damn!" Stone swore and pounded the steering wheel with the heel of his hand. "I knew I should have checked this car over while I was tuning up the Lincoln!"

"What's wrong with it?"

"It's overheating. I'd guess the radiator fluid level is low. I'll take a look."

While Stone stepped out of the Jeep, I checked my watch to see how much time we had before Wendy's flight arrived. We had an hour and ten minutes. I tried not to panic. By my estimate, we weren't more than twenty minutes from JFK Airport. Stone had worked on Harriet's car, so he must have some mechanical skills, I told myself. I bent my head and said a quick prayer that he'd have the Jeep running and back on the road within a few minutes. I looked up as Stone approached my window with something in his hand resembling a rubber snake.

"Here's our problem," he said in a disgusted voice.

"What's that?"

"It's the fan belt."

"Oh, my! It'd been running rough recently. I had it serviced just before I left Kansas. Kenny said the fan belt was still like new, or I would have had him replace it. He said the engine didn't need a complete tune-up yet. He just thought the air filter was probably clogged so he replaced it with a new one. It must have needed a complete tune-up."

"Kenny was probably correct. I doubt it needed a complete tune-up. It's possible it may need the timing adjusted, but that has nothing to do with this fan belt. See this smooth edge? Then it is jagged at the very edge." Stone held it up for my inspection. "Someone took a knife to it. It must've snapped in two a few minutes ago. Without the belt to run the fan, the engine overheats and shuts down the motor. It won't start again now until it cools off."

"We have over an hour before the flight is due," I said. "If we wait for it to cool off, could we make it—"

"No," Stone cut in with impatience. "After the engine cools down it will start, but we won't get far before it overheats again."

"But why would someone cut my fan belt? And who?"

"I don't know. Someone sabotaged your vehicle, I'm sure. I don't think it was a random act. Who knows you're here besides Harriet, Wendy, and me?"

"No one I'm aware of, Stone."

"Well, we'll have to worry about that later. Right now we need to find a way to get to the airport." Stone removed his cell phone from his belt clip and a plastic card from his wallet. Studying the card, he punched in a number. He spoke briefly into the phone, then dialed a second number. After he replaced the phone in the clip, he led me toward the grassy area beyond the shoulder, away from the Jeep and the heavy traffic on the busy interstate. The Jeep had stalled next to a green mile marker sign.

"Stand back here while I put the hood up on the Jeep and turn on the hazard lights. I have AAA on the way to tow the Jeep and a taxi coming to take us to the airport."

"Okay. Be careful."

I paced nervously on the shoulder while we waited for the taxi to arrive. By the time we were in the cab and on the way to JFK again, it was only a half hour before Wendy's flight arrived. I had always assumed all NYC taxi drivers drove ninety miles an hour and used curbs and sidewalks as passing lanes, often missing pedestrians by mere inches. In fact, I thought as a rule they ignored traffic laws altogether. So why'd we have to get the only law-abiding taxi driver in the whole darn city who was never within ten miles of exceeding the speed limit? Didn't this guy realize he was driving Miss Crazy, not Miss Daisy?

Our driver slowed down when anything crossed our path, whether it was ten feet or ten miles away. I was beginning to think he might have a depth-perception problem. Pedestrians darted across the street in front of us. At times they stood in the middle of the street, blocking traffic. I didn't actually want to see anyone get hurt, but I would have gladly nudged a few people out of the way with the cab's bumper.

Traffic slowed and became more congested as we neared the airport. Cars cut in and out in front of us and honked their horns incessantly as they swerved from lane to lane. We could hear a siren several blocks away. Before we knew it, traffic had come to a complete stop. I looked out the window and could see the airport up ahead. Stone saw the look of concern cross my face after I once again checked my watch.

"We'll get out here," he said to the cabby, as he handed the man forty dollars. Stone helped me out of the back seat and then held my hand as we zigzagged through traffic toward the terminal. Drivers honked and glared at us as if they wanted to nudge us out of the way with their bumpers. How rude!

We were winded by the time we entered the building, but we didn't slow down. I was surprised we weren't stopped and questioned by security until I noticed how many other agitated people were running at top speed through the terminal. It was over twenty minutes past the time the flight had been due to arrive. With any luck at all, the flight had been delayed.

When we reached the bank of televisions announcing arrival and departure times we stopped to scan the screens for Wendy's flight. Stone had been thinking along the same lines as I had. "Damn," he muttered. "Her flight was on time."

We took off running again. We were far from the baggage claim where Wendy would be waiting anxiously for us to appear. We were half an hour late. I knew she'd be concerned and upset if we weren't there to greet her.

"Come on," Stone said. "She'll have checked a suitcase, I assume, and she would have had to wait to pick it up."

"Yes, I'm sure she did," I said. I breathed a sigh of relief. Once again, I thanked God for having Stone with me. I needed someone who could think rationally and not panic in a situation such as this. "I taught her to pack lightly, but she'd still need more for this trip than she could possibly pack in a carry-on bag."

A few minutes later we were in front of the luggage claim conveyor belt. It was now almost forty minutes past the time Wendy's flight arrived. All passengers had claimed their bags and departed. One bag remained on the still-revolving belt. I didn't have to read the address tag to know it said "Wendy Pitt." I had given the luggage to Wendy last Christmas. The pretty blue-plaid suitcase looked ominous. My daughter was nowhere in sight.

Using Stone's phone, I called Wendy's cell phone number and left a panicky message on her voice mail. I tried Wendy and Clay's home phone. I let it ring at least a dozen times, but no one answered. I'm certain I used up several months' worth of airtime minutes on Stone's phone.

Stone had gone to speak with an airline representative. While

I waited for him to return, I paced nervously around the baggage claim area. I looked in every nook and cranny I could find—as if I truly expected Wendy to be hiding behind a trash can or something equally ridiculous.

Finally Stone returned. He had a concerned expression on his face. I nearly tackled him as he strode toward me. "What did they say?" I asked impatiently.

"Her name's listed on the flight's manifest, which would indicate only that she checked in luggage. But I'm sure it was after she'd checked her luggage when she called you. If Clay decided not to let her catch the flight, her name would still have been registered on the manifest and her luggage loaded onto the airplane," Stone said. He talked slowly and softly in an unsuccessful attempt to calm me. I was a complete wreck. "So the fact her name is on the manifest means very little at this point."

"What do we do now? We can't leave here until we're certain, without a single doubt, that Wendy's not in the airport somewhere. Maybe she just had to use the restroom. Yes! That's it! I'm sure that's all there is to it." Suddenly I felt a sense of relief. I was probably just overreacting because of the stress I was under. It could be nothing more than the fact Wendy had drunk too many complimentary beverages on the flight. "I'll check the ladies' room, you check the men's."

"What?"

"Oh, I'm sorry. I meant to say while I check the ladies' restroom, you could look around in other areas where she might have gone. We can meet back here in a half hour or so."

"Okay. First I'll go to the ticket counter, in case she wandered off looking for us and we somehow missed each other."

She wasn't in any of the restrooms in the terminal, at the ticket counter, or any other place Stone or I searched for her. I'd called her cell phone number and left another three or four messages, each sounding more hysterical than the previous ones. I'd also tried Wendy's home number several more times and was still unable to reach either her or Clay.

"Should I call the police?" I asked Stone.

"NYPD or Kansas City?"

"Kansas City, I guess. I'm sure now that she never boarded the plane."

"I doubt they'd do anything until she's been missing for at least twenty-four hours."

"Do you think Clay abducted her?" I asked.

"Why would you 'abduct' someone who is already with you?"

"I don't know," I said. I didn't know what to think at this point. I was too flustered to think clearly. "Do you think he'll hurt her?"

"No, Lexie, I don't. I can't imagine Clay is that stupid or apt to act that carelessly. You can only kill and assault so many wives before you start looking suspicious. My guess is that Wendy chickened out, not wanting to upset her husband—who she, incidentally, just discovered is not exactly the kind of man she believed him to be. Or Clay could have pressured her not to get on the plane because he wants to keep her away from the New York area, in the event she was to hear something about the Eliza Pitt case while she was here."

"That makes sense." I was beginning to feel a little better about the situation. Stone's rational thinking was starting to have a calming effect on me.

"I think you should try again to contact Wendy or Clay by phone while I go speak with security. I'll give them my cell phone number. I want them to be able to get in touch with us if necessary. I'll also have Wendy paged a couple times before we leave the airport." Stone sighed and ran his fingers through his hair before continuing. "We both need to calm down. Chances are we are getting upset over nothing."

"My guess is you'll get a phone call from her or reach her at her house this evening, and it will turn out that Wendy is just fine. Try not to panic, Lexie. Going to pieces now won't help the situation at all."

"Okay, you're right," I said. I knew Stone was trying to tell me I needed to pull myself together for Wendy's sake. "Thank you for being here for me."

"I can't think of any place I'd rather be." Stone kissed me very briefly on the lips and wrapped his arms around me as I cried quietly into the collar of his shirt. It was the first time he'd kissed me that way, and it was a bittersweet moment. It was one of the best, and one of the worst, moments of my life. I couldn't rest easy until I heard my daughter's voice and knew she was safe. Then maybe I could take the time to analyze the way I was beginning to feel about Stone.

Twenty-One

We took one last thorough look around the airport before Stone convinced me Wendy wasn't there and we should head back to the Camelot B&B in Schenectady. Wendy might be trying to get in touch with me at the inn, he reminded me. On our way toward the exit, I removed Wendy's suitcase from the baggage turnstile and then walked out of the terminal with it. Watching it circling aimlessly around on the belt by itself had been causing my stomach to feel tied up in knots. I was surprised when no one from security stopped to question me or insist I show my identification.

Stone had called for a taxi to pick us up at JFK and take us to the garage where my Jeep had been towed and a new fan belt had been installed. We were soon on our way out of the city. I worried that each mile Stone drove took me farther away from Wendy.

We rode back to the inn in near silence. Stone concentrated on driving, while I stared out the window. I was too concerned about the welfare of my daughter to make idle chatter, and yet I didn't want to voice my deepest fears. Stone seemed to understand how I felt and didn't try to press me. He reached over and patted my knee to comfort me.

When we finally pulled up in front of the Camelot B&B, I saw Harriet standing in the yard looking up at the porch. She had a hand on each hip and a cigarette dangling from her mouth. A cloud of smoke enveloped her like a swarm of hungry gnats.

On the front porch was one of the most attractive young men I'd ever seen. He reminded me of a popular movie star often featured in magazines that I subscribed to. With a brush in his hand, he was covering the railing and the spindles around the porch with a fresh coat of white paint. He waved as we pulled up to the curb.

Stone laughed and said, "I guess it didn't take long for Andy to fall under Harriet's spell."

Stone introduced me to his nephew. I liked Andy immediately. Although taller and slimmer than his uncle, Andy favored Stone in other ways. They had matching smiles and similar personalities. Andy was definitely a chip off Stone's block.

Andy finished painting the front porch while we unpacked our overnight bags. Then we enticed Harriet to walk across the street to the diner with us, and the four of us sat down to eat. We had decided to clue Harriet in on the current situation. It didn't seem to bother her that we'd been deceiving her all along. If the police, Clay, or Wendy called for us at the inn, we wanted Harriet to know why it was important to get the message to us immediately. Harriet surprised me with some remarkably good ideas as we all discussed how to proceed with the situation. I'd still been unable to reach Wendy or Clay on the phone.

After dinner, Stone paid the tab for all four of us. I'd been too upset to eat anything, so had nervously rearranged the food on my plate until it no longer resembled an appetizing meal. It was late as we walked back across the street to the inn. It had been a long, nerve-wracking day and I was worn out and emotionally drained, but still rattled. I climbed into bed, later amazed I'd fallen right to sleep.

★ ★ ★ ★ ★

Early the next morning, sitting on the back porch, Andy, Stone, and I sipped our "full-flavored" coffee. We were all startled when Stone's cell phone rang. Andy's eyes met mine and held as his uncle spoke into the phone.

"Stone Van Patten here." He listened a moment and nodded his head at Andy and me.

"Clay?" Stone asked. He paused to listen again. "Yes, I am a friend of your mother-in-law's. That was Lexie using my phone to call you."

I could only hear Stone's side of the conversation, but I listened intently, hoping to pick up clues as to what Clay was saying on the other end.

"We were to pick Wendy up at the airport yesterday, and she didn't come in on the flight. Her luggage did, but she didn't. We arrived a bit late due to car trouble, but we looked everywhere, and Wendy was nowhere to be found."

Stone stopped to listen again. I leaned closer but still couldn't understand Clay's words. It was obvious Clay was as concerned as we were about why Wendy didn't exit the plane at JFK airport.

"Yes—uh-huh—of course, Clay—I agree," Stone said.

Stone listened to Clay as a puzzled look crossed his face.

With a final, "Yes, I think that'd be a good idea," Stone replaced the phone on its clip on his belt. He reached over and clasped my hand in his.

"What's up?" Andy asked.

"Clay saw my number on his caller ID numerous times and wondered who was trying so hard to get in touch with him. He listened to the messages you left and called immediately. He told me Wendy did indeed board the plane. She had told him he could go on home, but he'd stayed until she had gotten on the plane, anyway, and he didn't leave until after it had taxied over to the runway. I believe him."

"But then—" Suddenly I was unable to continue my thought.

"Yes. I know what you're thinking. Wendy couldn't have been abducted at thirty thousand feet. Whatever occurred, it had to have been after she disembarked from the plane."

"What was Clay's reaction to the news that Wendy was missing?" Andy asked.

"Clay was alarmed and upset, but not overly shocked by the idea she could have been abducted at this end from the JFK airport. He made a curious statement when I first told him she hadn't been at the airport when we arrived a bit late."

"What'd he say?" Andy and I asked in unison.

"He said, 'Oh no, not again.' There was genuine agony in his voice too."

"Talking about Eliza, wasn't he?" I asked.

"Yes, I think so. I asked what he meant by his remark, and when Clay realized what he'd said, he replied, 'Oh nothing. Never mind.' "

"What do you think now, Stone?"

"I believe him, Lexie. I really do. He seemed totally surprised and sincerely upset. I don't think he's responsible for Wendy's disappearance. Perhaps someone in New York has a personal vendetta against him."

"Why?"

"Who knows? Anyway, he's booking a flight and heading out here. I told him I thought it was a good idea. I think there's a connection between Wendy's disappearance and Eliza's abduction. We need to buckle down and see what we can find out from any and every source today. The sooner we can find Wendy, the better. First thing I'll do is call the NYPD to report the incident."

"I'll help in any way I can, Uncle Stone," Andy volunteered. Then he turned toward me and noticed the look of sheer terror on my face. "Don't worry, Lexie. We'll find her."

"Detective Glick?" I said into the phone.

"Yes?"

"This is Lexie Starr."

"Lexie Starr, freelance writer?"

"Yes."

"Can I help you?" I noticed he didn't sound overly thrilled.

"Well, yes . . . uh, I was wondering if you had made any new progress on the Eliza Pitt case?"

"Nothing more than what I'm sure you saw on television. Anything beyond that would be classified information I'd be unable to share with you."

"Why do you dislike me so much, detective?"

"I don't dislike you, Ms. Starr. I don't even know you. I take my position seriously. I can't tell everything I know—about every case I'm involved in—to everyone I meet. That wouldn't be very professional, now would it?"

I sighed. Detective Glick was a very hard nut to crack. I was wasting my time trying to get any information out of him.

"I guess not. Thanks anyway."

"Sheriff Crabb. May I help you?" I heard on the other end of the line.

"Yes, Sheriff Crabb, this is Lexie Starr. We met about a week ago. I'm the lady writing the novel about the Eliza Pitt case. Do you remember me?"

"Well, I declare," he answered. "Of course I remember you. I surely do. One doesn't often get to meet a honest-to-goodness gen-u-wine author like yourself."

"Thanks," I said, amused by his effusiveness. I felt a twinge of guilt for deceiving him and getting him excited about a book and movie that would never materialize. "I enjoyed meeting you too. The reason I'm calling you this morning is to see if you've made any new discoveries in the Pitt case."

"Yes, ma'am, I'm happy to report we've made some progress in that case lately. Your friend, Detective Glick, made an interesting discovery a few days ago. Found the actual site where the lady was killed. Apparently she was later moved to the site where that hiker kid found her. You may have seen the news report on this."

"Yes, I did, as a matter of fact. Could you show me the site the detective discovered where Eliza Pitt was actually killed?"

"Nah, wish I could, but I don't rightly know where that is yet. Sure sorry, ma'am."

Gee, this guy is a wealth of information, I thought. It appeared the sheriff was still not entrusted with any classified information. If I couldn't get any useful info out of him, I'd have to use him to get it another way.

"Hmmm . . . say, I've got an idea. My boyfriend's an officer with the Myrtle Beach, South Carolina, police force. He's been assisting me with my research for this book I'm writing. I know he'd be honored to help you with your investigation. Just for the sake of the novel, you know. It'd be good experience for him to have you as a mentor. And I hate to admit it, but Detective Glick is a bit out of sorts with me right now. He seems to think I should base the novel and potential screenplay on him and his involvement in this case. However, I believe it would be more exciting, and more appropriate, to highlight you. After all, you are the authority on this murder case now."

I knew Sheriff Crabb's weakness, and I was not above exploiting it.

"That's mighty kind of you, Ms. Starr. I'm sure you know what would be best for your book. And I suppose it'd be okay if your policeman friend—er—uh—Officer—"

"Officer Van Patten."

"Thanks. Yeah, I'd be happy to let Officer Van Patten tag along. You're right. It could be of great benefit to him to see how I handle this case. I'm always willing to help a fellow lawman learn the ropes." Amused, I visualized Sheriff Crabb rocking back and forth on his heels and toes again, with one hand holding the phone and the thumb of his other hand hooked in his belt. I could barely suppress my laughter.

"That's mighty kind of you, sheriff. To expedite matters, perhaps you could call Detective Glick and have him meet you and Officer Van Patten there. He can take the two of you to the actual murder site. Because of your professionalism and competency, I'm sure you'll want to take photographs, and do your own investigative work at the murder scene, anyway. This would be ideal timing for you too."

"True, very true. Got to cover all the bases, ma'am. That's how we professionals operate, you know. Leave no stone unturned—that's always been my motto."

"Of course. I'm very impressed, sheriff."

"Ah, shucks, ma'am. Just doing my job. I'll set up a meeting with the Schenectady detective, Glick. Have Officer Van Patten meet me at my office at two o'clock this afternoon. We can follow Detective Glick out to the crime scene in my squad car."

"Yes, that'd be fine. And, Sheriff Crabb?"

"Yes, ma'am?"

"Perhaps you shouldn't mention my name around Detective Glick at all. He is already jealous of your role in all of this, you know. I don't want to fan the flames and cause any friction," I said. "It's probably best that Glick doesn't know about my connection to Officer Van Patten. He's already upset enough about being upstaged by you."

"I understand. I'll try to keep your name out of the conversation, Ms. Starr."

"Thanks. And I'll make sure that Officer Van Patten is at your office at two."

Stone left in his Corvette to meet Sheriff Crabb. Andy decided to paint Harriet's back porch while we waited for his uncle to return. I paced restlessly because I couldn't relax. Wendy was on my mind constantly, and I felt like it was my own interference that had placed her in her current predicament, a predicament I didn't care to think about too much. Who had my daughter and what were they doing to her? The possibilities were too frightening to dwell on, so I tried to distract myself with other things.

I even welcomed the distraction of eating breakfast. I picked up my fork and absentmindedly began picking at the platter of poached eggs and toast Harriet set before me. It could have been a plate full of grub worms for all the attention I paid to the food Harriet had prepared. The feisty old proprietor seemed to sense I needed something to do to keep me busy until I heard from Stone.

"After ya done with ya breakfast, why don't ya go back and see old Nitwit Pitt agin?" Harriet asked. "No sense wearing out me floors and being under me feet all day. Ya ne'er know. Ya jest might git something useful outta the ol' nutcase."

"Hey, that's a good idea, Harriet. Thanks. I'll take her a few more books. I'm not sure she'd be ready for more candy yet. It hasn't been that long since I gave her ten pounds of chocolates."

"Ha! Are ya blind, girl? She had dem candies et up befer you left the parking lot, iffing ya ask me."

I knew Harriet was exaggerating, but she did have a valid point. Wanda Pitt did not get to be her size by eating sensibly. I'd pick up one more five-pound box of chocolates and several Harlequins on my way to Serenity Village. It would kill a little time and keep my mind off what might be happening to Wendy.

And who knows? Maybe Harriet was right and I would pick up some useful tidbit of information.

"Take dem pictures with ya, why don't ya?" Harriet said as I rinsed my empty platter and set it in the sink. Stone had shown Harriet and Andy the reprints while we ate supper at the Union Street Diner the night before.

TWENTY-TWO

Andy gave me his cell phone and promised to call me just as soon as he'd heard from his uncle. He encouraged me to try and relax in the meantime.

"Uncle Stone said he'd call on Harriet's number for just this very reason." Andy told me. "He knew you wouldn't be able to sit still this morning while you waited to hear from him. I'm restless myself. That's why I decided to paint Harriet's back porch."

"Is that the only reason, Andy?" I teased.

"Well, no. It's also because I had quite a lot of leftover white paint, and Harriet didn't want to see it go to waste. I doubt she wanted to waste the 'elbow grease' I was offering either."

Andy chuckled in an endearing manner that reminded me of Stone. I was surprised that somehow, in the very depths of despair, I could still find humor in life's everyday situations. Once again, I found myself laughing to keep from crying.

On the way to Serenity Village, I stopped at the pharmacy to pick up the care package items for Clay's mother. I recalled her comment about celebrating a birthday this week and had a sudden desire to try and make it special for her so it would not be the lonely, depressing event she'd anticipated.

I found a large wicker basket and two bright, colorful silk scarves to line the bottom. To fill the basket I bought the books and chocolates, along with a brush and comb, several tubes of lipstick, a manicure set, two bottles of nail polish, and a selection of lotions, shampoos, and perfumes. I'd tell Wanda she deserved to be pampered on her birthday, and this gift was a collection of self-pampering tools. With any luck at all she'd utilize the items and take a little more interest in her appearance.

I selected an appropriate greeting card that complemented the basket before proceeding to the checkout counter. The clerk at the pharmacy recommended a bakery a few blocks away. There I selected a small chocolate birthday cake, and had the top decorated with icing spelling out "Happy Birthday, Wanda." One large candle was placed in the center. Hopefully, Wanda had at least one friend at the center to share her cake and help celebrate her birthday.

There was a different young girl at the front desk of Serenity Village from the first time I'd visited, so I informed her I was Wanda's niece, Clara Pitt, and headed down the hallway to Wanda's room with my armload of goodies. Under the birthday basket was a folder with the photos we'd had reprinted from Jake's negatives.

A becoming smile brightened Wanda's face when she saw the cake and basket. I realized Wanda had probably been a very beautiful woman at one time. She could be very attractive again, if she made an effort to take better care of herself.

"Carla! How good to see you again!"

"Hello, Wanda. It's Clara, Clara Ransfield. I thought I'd drop by to wish you a happy birthday." I set the cake on her kitchen counter and handed her the basket.

The look on Wanda's face told me I had never given anyone a gift as appreciated as the one I'd handed her. I was thankful that Harriet had suggested the idea of visiting Clay's mother again.

I didn't mention to Wanda that the cake I'd bought was made

of sugar-free chocolate, with low-fat, low-calorie vanilla icing. I could see no purpose in adding to her weight problems. The box of chocolates was also endorsed by the American Diabetes Association and contained a sugar substitute. She was certain to notice when she opened the box, but maybe she'd discover they were a tasty alternative to the real thing.

I chatted with Wanda about trivial matters for several minutes and watched while she inspected all of the treats in her basket. She agreed that maybe she could benefit from a little self-pampering and told me she was anxious to try out all the items I'd brought for her. Wanda thanked me effusively as she fawned over each item in the basket.

"Bringing me all these nice things was so thoughtful of you, Claire. I really appreciate your kindness. By the way, have you seen Clayton, my son?" Wanda asked, abruptly.

I wasn't sure how she could have expected me to see him, or even where to find him, but I welcomed the opportunity to switch the subject over to discussing Clay. I had to remind myself that Wanda Pitt had lived in a home for the mentally ill for many years. She might have forgotten that, to her, I was just an administrator at the Serenity Village facility. After all, she couldn't even remember my name for five minutes.

"No, Wanda, I haven't seen your son. But I've recently visited with an old roommate of his, named Jake Jacoby. Do you know Jake?"

"No, can't say I ever heard of him."

I opened my folder and pulled out the picture we'd had enlarged of Jake and Clay. I handed it to Wanda, and she smiled as she stared at the photograph.

"That's my boy, Clayton Oliver! Don't recognize the other one, though. Is this one the roommate you visited?" Wanda asked, pointing at Jake in the photo.

"Yes, that's Jake Jacoby."

"What's all that stuff on his face?" Wanda asked as she moved the photo closer to her face and studied the earring in Jake's eyebrow. She'd been in this facility for so long that I doubted she'd witnessed the recent trends of the younger generation.

"Body piercings. It's a new fad. A way for young folks to express themselves—like tattoos. I have to admit I don't see the attraction of it, but maybe that's just my age showing."

"How old are you, by the—?"

"—Forty-eight. Probably close to your own—"

"Yeah, I turned fifty yesterday. I never thought I'd see the day that I'd live to be fifty. But stranger things have happened, I suppose."

I smiled and nodded. I thought it must have been a very sad day for Wanda. Fifty was a milestone. To reach the milestone of a half century in age, without the company of another human being, must be a very lonely experience.

I was glad I'd purchased a new apron for Harriet at the pharmacy, in order to thank her for her recommendation that I visit Wanda once again. I planned to stop at a silk-screening shop on the way back to the inn to have it personalized. "Welcome to Harriet's kitchen" it would read across the front. It would be a time-consuming distraction for me.

Wanda grunted and repositioned herself on the sofa, reached across the coffee table, and picked up the other photos in my folder.

"Do you mind if I have a look at these?"

I could see she was anxious to view more photos of her son, Clayton, whom she'd said she hadn't seen in many years. I wished I had a stack to offer her, instead of just the two photos. Next time I visited I'd bring her one of Clay in a tuxedo, taken at his and Wendy's wedding in August. She'd be proud of what a handsome man her son was today. I could surely concoct a believable story to explain why I had all the photos.

"Sure. There's only one more of Clayton, however," I said, as I picked out the photo of Clay behind the slaughtered moose. "Big moose, huh? Do you happen to recognize the cabin behind Clayton in this photo?"

"No, never saw it before," she said, shaking her head. She looked at the next photo in the stack and beamed broadly. "Well, I'll be damned! Here's a picture of Ma and Pa! This had to have been taken shortly before Pa died. What a wonderful photo of the two of them! Oh, how I wish I had a copy of this one."

I looked down at the photo of the elderly couple I'd mistakenly assumed were Jake's grandparents. "This is your mother and father?"

"Yes." There were tears of joy in Wanda's eyes.

Wanda stared at the photo for what seemed like several minutes. Eventually, she set the photo down on the coffee table and picked up the rest of the reprints from the pile.

"Here's Clay's first car," she said. "He saved his money and was so proud when he could finally afford to buy this convertible. He used to take me on rides around town in it, with the top down. Oh, and look here. It's his old dog, Buddy. Surely Buddy is gone by now. Buddy and Clayton were inseparable when they were both young."

It suddenly occurred to me the stack of photos we'd found in Jake Jacoby's house had belonged to Clay, not to Jake. I thought back to a conversation I'd had with Wendy on the phone while she was still attending college and had just begun "officially" dating Clay. I vaguely remembered her mentioning that Clay had sold his old car and bought the new Avalanche truck. Apparently it was the Mustang that Wendy had referred to, and Clay had sold it to his roommate, Jake.

I wasn't sure if, or how, this information would help us in any way. And I didn't think I was apt to get anything else out of my visit with Wanda that would be beneficial. I wanted to stop and get Harriet's apron personalized and be back at the inn by the time Stone called. I spent a few more minutes with Wanda before giving the excuse that I had to get back to work in the administrative offices of the care center. I would be back to see her soon, I promised. It was a promise I intended to keep.

As I was preparing to leave, Wanda picked up the enlargement of Clay and Jake for one last look. She grinned as she handed it back to me.

"He sure has become a handsome man, hasn't he? 'Course he was good-looking as a kid too. Took after his daddy in that respect. Homer's always been a looker. Got to give him that much anyway."

"How old was Homer when he . . . uh . . . died?" I asked, hesitantly. Wanda's use of the present tense had confused me.

"Died? Hell, Caroline, Homer ain't dead, just locked up. He's still in the pen, last I heard."

"The pen?" What happened to the damn fool bleeding to death on the kitchen floor after he ran right into the butcher knife? I wondered.

"Yeah," Wanda said. "Someone told me a few years ago he got sent up the river for robbing a liquor store. Shot the fellow behind the counter. Didn't kill him, but the poor fellow's still got a hunk of lead in his skull. Pretty much a vegetable now, from what I hear."

"But . . . but, Wanda, didn't you tell me you killed Homer in self-defense, and Clayton witnessed the whole thing?"

"Now, Cora, don't be silly. Why would I tell you something as crazy as all that?"

Oh my goodness, Wanda. Because you are crazy, that's why! What had I been thinking? Just because Wanda sounded intelligent and competent most of the time didn't mean anything she told me was the truth. There had to have been a good reason for her to live in this facility for the last sixteen years. After all, they didn't normally institutionalize perfectly sane people in homes for the mentally ill. Occasionally, perhaps, but not very often.

"I'm sorry, Wanda. I must have misunderstood."

I was shaking my head in disbelief as I gathered up the photos and prepared to leave. Everything I thought I knew about Clay's childhood, and about his parents, had just flown out the window. If nothing else, I still believed the old couple in the one photo was Wanda's parents, and the photos we'd had reprinted had belonged to Clay, not Jake.

"So long now—uh, what was your name again?"

Carlene? Connie? Wanda had called me so many different names that, for a moment, even I couldn't remember the one I'd invented. "It's, er, Clara. Yeah, that's it."

"Oh, yes, it's Clara, of course. Be careful in the hallways, Clara," Wanda cautioned, as I opened the door of her apartment. "Thanks again for the gifts and coming to see me."

I said good-bye and then wished her a happy birthday once again—a birthday I now realized could have just as likely been four months ago, as yesterday. For some inane reason, I looked around, as if concerned about being pursued by Wanda's purple, one-eyed monsters on the way to the parking lot.

Twenty-Three

"Lexie?"

"Yes?" I said to Andy, as I spoke to him on his own cell phone.

"Uncle Stone just called. Detective Glick took him and the sheriff out to the murder scene, as promised. He thought maybe you'd want to see it with your own eyes."

"He's right, I do."

"He asked me to bring you to the Sinclair station in DeKalb. He said he'd meet us there, and we'd all take your Jeep out to the site."

"I'm on my way back to the inn right now, Andy. I'll be there in less than ten minutes."

"This is a pretty remote area, isn't it?" I asked Stone as the three of us stood in the dense forest, in an infrequently traversed section of the Adirondack Mountain Range.

"Yes. According to Glick it's not a very popular area because of the dense underbrush and the abundance of stinging nettles."

"Did he or Sheriff Crabb happen to mention why or how Eliza's body got moved to the location where Crowfoot eventually discovered it?" Andy asked.

"No. They are both baffled by how or why that occurred. They've considered the idea a mountain lion may have dragged her there, but the forensic scientist nixed the possibility. The body showed no bite marks, or anything of that nature."

"See those dozen or so stones over by the large pine tree?"

164

Stone pointed toward the tree.

"Yes," I said, as Andy and I both looked in its direction.

"That's where Eliza's sweatshirt was found, and also her blood, which was splattered all over one of the stones. That particular stone was taken in for DNA testing. Glick thinks it was most likely the blunt object used to kill Eliza."

Stone and Andy wandered off to inspect an old abandoned cottage they spied about three or four hundred feet on the other side of my Jeep. I walked about a hundred feet in the opposite direction, to the assortment of stones that Stone had pointed out.

I sat down with my back against an old tree trunk. The tree had probably fallen many years earlier. I sat quietly, thinking about Eliza's gruesome death, and wondering what kind of sick individual could do such a horrific thing to anybody, much less a pregnant woman. There were tears in my eyes and sweat on my brow as I thought about Wendy being in the hands of the same individual who had perpetrated this crime.

I was absentmindedly picking up the stones one by one and piling them up beside me. "Leave no stone unturned"—Sheriff Crabb's motto—went through my mind as I dug out the last of the scattered stones. It was tough to dislodge since it was half-buried in the hardened mud. I placed the stone on top of the pile beside me and noticed the sun glint off something shiny where the stone had been. The shiny object was half-covered in fine dirt. As I reached over and picked up the shiny object, a large hand clamped down over my wrist and jerked my body sideways. I let out an involuntary scream in response, just as another hand covered my mouth.

"What are you doing here?" I heard a familiar voice ask.

I looked up into the square, angry face of Detective Glick. He slowly released his right hand from my wrist, and then removed the left one that was covering my mouth.

"What are *you* doing here?" I countered. "We thought you'd left."

"I came back to pick up an exposed film cartridge that I'd left on a log back by where your Jeep is parked. Did I hear you say 'we'? Are you the other half of Officer Van Patten, by any chance?" he asked in an irritated voice. It had just dawned on him he'd been tricked, and he wasn't happy about it.

"I have a right to be here, detective."

"No, you don't, Ms. Starr. This is a crime scene—the site of a murder investigation—not just the scene for your next chapter. A young woman lost her life here, savagely. How would you feel if you were a member of the family that's been devastated by her death? Would you like to have writers crawling about the murder scene, interfering with the investigation, and contaminating potential evidence?"

"I am a member of the family that's been affected, Detective Glick! That's why I'm here. I'm almost certain the person who killed Eliza Pitt has abducted my daughter, the second Mrs. Pitt. Her name is Wendy, and she's now married to Clayton Pitt."

"What? Clayton Pitt has remarried? He married your daughter and now she's missing?" Glick seemed overwhelmed by this new turn of events. "So, you're not just here because you're a writer, Ms. Starr?"

"Please call me Lexie, Detective Glick."

"Okay, Lexie. I'm Ron." He motioned for me to continue.

"I'm not a writer at all, Ron. I told you a lie because I thought maybe I could get some information from you, but, as you well know, I was wrong."

"Why didn't you just tell me the truth? I would've helped you had I known the real reason you wanted information about the case."

"I didn't want anyone to know I was here in New York,

investigating the murder. I didn't want any information to get back to my new son-in-law, Clayton Pitt, whom I feared was the killer. But now it has anyway, and my daughter, Wendy, has vanished. We've come to the conclusion Clayton is most likely not involved in her abduction, but there is a connection there somewhere we haven't figured out yet." I began to cry in frustration. I'd been controlling my emotions quite admirably until now.

"You need to tell me everything you know. We'll work together and see what we can come up with by putting our heads together. Here comes Officer Van Patten. I want to hear the whole story from both of you. Oh, I suppose he's not really an officer. He—"

"He is—"

"—and the younger guy with him? They're running. They probably heard you scream."

"Yes, I'm sure they did. Stone's a reserve officer in South Carolina. Stone and I are just friends. The younger man is his nephew, Andy," I said. I looked up as Stone and Andy reached our location. Stone was panting for breath. Andy was hardly winded. They both inquired if I was okay and wanted to know what was happening. I explained briefly after introducing Ron to Andy. Detective Glick acknowledged Stone and shook hands with Andy. "Lexie has explained the true situation to me. I need the whole story so we can get cracking and locate her daughter."

Ron pulled a notebook and pen from his pocket and jotted down notes while he asked us questions about Clayton and Wendy. Then he pulled out a radio and called for an APB on Wendy. I described my daughter as best I could and showed Ron several photos from my wallet. He chose the most recent one to take with him so he could have fliers printed and distributed. I began to have a higher opinion of my former nemesis and was glad that Ron and I were now on the same side.

When Stone helped me to my feet I remembered the shiny object still enclosed in my fist. I opened up my hand to reveal a hatpin in the shape of a four-leafed clover. Across the top was inscribed "Shamrock Club—Seattle, Washington," and along the bottom it read, "Come on in and get lucky."

"Seattle?" Ron asked.

"Rod Crowfoot!" Stone, Andy, and I all answered in unison.

Like charms on a bracelet, the hatpins were meant to show where Rod had been. Rod had been at the murder scene—before he'd been at the location where he'd "discovered" Eliza's body. Who was Rod Crowfoot, and how was he connected to Clay or Eliza Pitt? Why would he want to kill Clay's wife? Most importantly, where was he now?

We climbed into the Jeep and followed Ron Glick back to the DeKalb sheriff's office, where we brought Sheriff Crabb up to date on the latest development. Sheriff Crabb was more intelligent and competent than he sometimes appeared to be. When he acted star-struck by my status as a successful author, I found it difficult to believe he'd been placed in such an authoritative position.

Sheriff Crabb surprised me now by suggesting that if Rod had one of the club's hatpins, it might be one of his favorite hangouts, or at least may have been a place he frequented at one time. If that were the case, he surmised, then someone at the club might remember him. We agreed, and Stone reached for his cell phone on the belt clip.

At Ted Crabb's insistence, Stone pocketed his cell phone and used the sheriff's desk phone instead. First he dialed 1-4-1-1 for national directory assistance and was given the phone number for the Shamrock Club in Seattle. He asked the operator to connect him. Ron reached over and pushed the speaker-phone button on the telephone so we could all listen in on the conversation.

"Shamrock Club," a young man's voice said over the speak-erphone.

"Good afternoon. Is the owner available?" Stone asked.

"Dunno. I'll go see if Ray's here. Hang on a minute."

We stood around and waited for several minutes. We had begun to think the young man had forgotten Stone was waiting on the phone when an older man's deep voice erupted from the speakerphone and resonated around the cramped room.

"This is Ray. May I help you?"

"Ray, this is Stone Van Patten. I'm trying to locate an old friend of mine named Rod Crowfoot. I'm fairly certain Rod used to patronize your club. Do you recall the man I'm talking about?"

"Sure I do. He worked for me as a male stripper for several years. I haven't seen him in quite awhile though, Mr. Van Patten, so I doubt I can be of much help to you."

"When was the last time you saw Rod?"

"If you're a friend of his, you probably remember when that foster father of his died, don't you? You know, the guy that Rod called Uncle Bill?"

"Uh-huh," Stone answered noncommittally. "Go on."

"Well, Rod moved back to New York to be near the property Bill left him—that little place in the mountains with the log cabin on it. Bill always went out there in the fall to hunt deer. Anyway, I haven't seen Rod since he moved back there, and that was three years ago, I'd say. Another one of my strippers just moved back East a couple of months ago to try and rekindle a relationship with Rod. I think he told me Rod lived in Boston now. The two of them had been an item for a long time, but split up when Rod caught Wade cheating on him with another guy. Apparently Wade was successful, because he hasn't come back to Seattle yet."

The five of us stood in a circle with our mouths hanging open in astonishment. A big piece of the puzzle had just fallen into place. The Shamrock Club was another gay bar. And Rod Crowfoot had changed his identity to become Jake Jacoby.

TWENTY-FOUR

I gave Detective Glick Jake's address in Boston, where Stone and I had made our exterminating visit. Ron raised his eyebrows in astonishment. I knew he was surprised I knew Jake's address, but he made no comment as he called his office. He spoke to his superior for a few minutes and then was transferred over to the sheriff's office in Boston. He spoke to a Detective Sharp. Sharp arranged to have a SWAT team surround Jacoby's residence in the event Jake was holding Wendy there.

We sat around in the DeKalb sheriff's office for the next half hour, nervously waiting for a return call from the Boston detective. We all drank several cups of really bad coffee and tried to decide on a plan of action. I'd attempted to contact Clay again on his cell phone, but I got his voice mail instead.

"Clay, this is Lexie," I said to his voice mail recorder. "Call me as soon as you can at Stone's cell phone number."

I recited the number into the phone and took a deep breath. I wanted to give Clay an advance warning. Hopefully he'd begin thinking about anything he could tell us that might be beneficial in locating Wendy. He'd find out soon enough we knew all about the murder case involving his first wife. It was time for him to come clean with us and tell us all he knew about the situation. "We think now that it's Jake Jacoby who has abducted Wendy," I said. "Jake Jacoby is actually Rod Crowfoot, the hiker who discovered Eliza's body. I'll fill you in on everything that's happened when you return my call. Please call me ASAP."

I'd noticed Sheriff Crabb had been shooting me questioning glances for a while. It suddenly occurred to me that, although he knew that my daughter was married to Clayton Pitt and she'd disappeared, he hadn't quite figured out how "Lexie Starr, writer" figured into the whole equation. I crossed the room to speak to him. He was sitting behind his desk, so I crouched down beside him.

"Forgive me, Ted?"

"Ma'am?"

"I guess you've figured out by now I'm not really writing a novel about the Eliza Pitt case. I'm sorry I had to deceive you, Ted."

"S'okay," the sheriff replied with a shrug. "I understand. So what are you really writing about, Ms. Starr?"

"No, I meant I'm not a writer at all, Ted. I'm just a concerned mother, doing whatever it takes to protect, and now find, my daughter."

"Oh—yeah—sure. Of course. No apology necessary, Ms. Starr."

"Thank you, Sheriff. I really do appreciate all you've done to help me."

"Ah, shucks, ma'am. I'm just doing my job." He looked away with a disappointed expression on his face. Then he slowly turned back my way. "Does this mean that Sly Stallone, and the whole movie deal, is off too?"

"Damn! The house is empty," Detective Glick said. He replaced the handset in the cradle after thanking Detective Sharp for his assistance. "We need to find out where he's hiding. I'd bet the farm Crowfoot's got Wendy with him at the log cabin, and he's holding her as a hostage, something to use as negotiating material. At least, I hope that's what he's doing. I sure wish we could make contact with Clay so we could find out where the cabin's located."

Stone rose from the chair he'd been sitting on and said, "Let's pay another visit to the Fantasy Club. If he's not there, at least Baines McFarland should be. McFarland may know where Jake is or, at least, how long it's been since he's reported for work."

"How will we get there?" Ron asked. Boston was a long way from Schenectady, and there just wasn't time for us to drive there.

Stone thought for a moment and then turned to his nephew. "Andy, would you mind flying us all to Boston in your plane?"

"I'd be happy to, Uncle Stone. I'll call ahead and have the plane fueled up and ready to go. I have a friend, Joe, who's an aviation engineer. He lives close to the airport. I'm sure Joe will run up there and take care of it for me."

Sheriff Crabb had to remain at his post, but the remaining four of us piled into Glick's squad car and headed for the town of Glenville, where the Schenectady County Airport was located.

Ron flicked on his flashing lights and siren after we'd taken the exit on to Route 50. "Every hour that goes by could be critical, I'm afraid. The quicker we find Jake and Wendy, the better. I don't want to waste a minute if we can help it," he said.

His words sent a chill up my spine. I couldn't help thinking about the consequences of finding Wendy too late. At least it kept me from thinking about the carnage sure to result when Ron's police car wiped out going one hundred miles an hour down the highway. I closed my eyes so I wouldn't see the fence posts flashing by outside my window, like spokes in a spinning bicycle wheel. And I had thought riding with Stone in his Corvette was terrifying. Now that ride seemed sedate in comparison. Thankfully, it was a short trip to the airport and we arrived there safely.

Minutes later we were boarding Andy's plane, a five-passenger Cessna. As we strapped ourselves in, Andy began taxiing down the runway. We were promptly given permission by the air traffic controller to take off. The plane lifted off the runway smoothly and gained altitude rapidly.

Above the roar of the engines, I could hear Andy say he planned to land at a small executive airport in Boston. He'd already arranged to have a rental car waiting for us. I was impressed by his foresightedness. Like his uncle, he was efficient and organized and preferred not to leave anything to chance. I found myself wishing Wendy had met and married a man like Andy, instead of Clay. Andy had a lean, but athletic, physique, a clean-cut hairstyle, and startling blue eyes—the kind that'd entice someone to take a second glance. Long, dark eyelashes that would surely make any woman envious set off his blue eyes. However, Andy's best feature, like Stone's, was his smile. He had a broad smile highlighted by straight, white teeth. Andy's only apparent imperfection was a scar running diagonally through his left eyebrow. Stone had told me the scar was the result of a playground accident when Andy was seven. Somehow the scar only seemed to add character to his tanned, strong-featured face.

Andy seemed to sense I was studying him as he handled the controls. He turned around in the pilot's seat and smiled at me. He tried to comfort me like he had several times before. "We'll find her, Lexie. Don't worry. Sit back and relax while you have the chance."

"Get off my property!" Baines McFarland said, pointing his finger in Stone's face. "Smith and Wesson, my ass. Do you think I'm some kind of idiot? I may just have you arrested for impersonating an officer. I happen to know you and 'Officer Smith' are not really police officers, any more than you're exterminators."

"I am a police officer, McFarland, albeit just a reserve officer in Myrtle Beach," Stone said. "But my real name is Van Patten, Stone Van Patten. My first visit with you was tied in with an undercover operation. We couldn't risk having Jacoby find out we were investigating him. It appears Jake has now abducted my partner's daughter. It's critical we locate him immediately."

McFarland looked over toward me but made no comment.

"Why'd you make that comment about us not being exterminators?" Stone asked.

"I called the NYPD Homicide Division. They told me they'd never heard of you or your partner here," Baines said, nodding in my direction. "I called there because I had thought of something else I wanted to tell you, and I couldn't reach you on the cell phone number you'd given me."

"And what was it you wanted to tell us?"

"Never mind that now. I'm not telling you a damn thing. I don't have to answer your questions, Van Patten."

Detective Glick motioned Stone to move aside, and he stepped up in front of Baines McFarland. Ron Glick was an imposing figure to begin with, but he was even more intimidating when he had a person backed into a corner the way he now had McFarland. Ron thrust his ID badge in McFarland's face and held it there against the man's nose.

"I'm Glick. Detective Ron Glick. You'll answer my questions, McFarland, or I'll haul your worthless hide into the station."

"Oh yeah? On what charges?"

"On obstruction of justice for starters. And then we'll work our way up to accessory to murder, and aiding and abetting a criminal. If there's a charge for being a moron, we'll throw that one in too."

Ron was angry and relentless. I could tell it wasn't merely an act to persuade McFarland to talk. He'd taken several steps forward and had McFarland standing with his back against the wall. Ron towered over the diminutive club owner. As he glared down at McFarland, his square face resembled a block of concrete in its intensity. McFarland had rivulets of sweat streaming down from his forehead, and he was wringing his hands in apprehension. He glanced right and then left, as if looking for an escape route.

In an unexpected display of bravado and contempt, McFarland placed his hands on his hips and looked up into Ron's face. "I guess you'll just have to haul my worthless hide to the station, Glick. I don't know anything about any murder, and I've certainly had no involvement in one," he said in a defiant tone. "I don't know anything about the murder of that Pitt gal. I told your friends that the first time they came in here and harassed me. I'm getting pretty tired of you clowns coming onto my property and accusing me of being an accessory to a crime I don't know anything about."

"Forget the murder for right now. We're more concerned about the current situation involving the abduction. I want to know everything you know about Jake Jacoby."

"I don't know anything about him. You want to know about Jacoby, talk to him, not me! He works for me. That's all I can tell you."

"Where is he?"

"He's not here." Baines tried to scoot out from around Ron, but he didn't get far.

Glick grabbed the front of McFarland's perfectly pressed shirt, lifted him off his feet, and slammed him up against the wall. He now had McFarland's complete attention, and everyone else's too. "I didn't ask if he was here. I asked you where he was. Now, where is he?"

"Get your hands off me, Glick, or I'll sue you for police brutality."

"You'll tell me where Jacoby is right this minute, or there won't be enough left of you to sue anybody." Ron's voice was low and steely. It was clear his words were not a threat. They were a promise. He'd pinned McFarland up against the wall again, and the smaller man's feet were suspended off the ground.

McFarland weighed his options quickly and chose self-preservation over self-righteousness. Ron released Baines as the man reluctantly began to talk.

"Jacoby hasn't reported to work for the last couple of days. I don't know why, or where he's at, I swear. He lives over on the seven hundred block of Eighth Street. I've tried calling him several times, but he hasn't answered his phone or returned my calls. Wade, the new backup stripper—Jake's boyfriend—is on sick leave. I wouldn't be surprised if Wade's got AIDS. He seems a bit promiscuous. But whatever—it leaves me in a real bind. Jake's always been extremely reliable until now. Never missed a day's work that I can recall. He's gullible and a little too naive at times, but he doesn't impress me as a killer or a kidnapper."

"Do you know where we could find Wade?" Stone asked.

"No, I don't know much about him. He hasn't been working here long; just moved here from Seattle not long ago. He was in the hospital last I knew." Baines was answering Stone and Ron's questions, but it was apparent he wasn't going to volunteer a lot of information unless pressured.

"Which hospital?"

"That New England Medical Center over on Washington Street. Tufts, I think it's called—or something like that."

"What's Wade's last name?" Stone asked.

"Williams."

"Okay, thanks. Once again, how did you know my partner and I had pretended to be exterminators?"

Baines glanced at Ron, but quickly turned back to Stone to answer his question. I could understand why it made him nervous to take his eyes off Detective Glick.

"When I found out there were no Detectives Smith and Wesson working for the NYPD, I decided to tell Jake two people were here impersonating police officers and asking questions about him. I described you two to Jake, and he said it fit the description of the pair that had sprayed his house for spiders earlier the same day. He told me he'd thought at the time there was something odd about the whole exterminating episode. Said he'd never heard of an exterminator showing up on the job in a Corvette. I gave him the cell phone number you'd given me and also told him you said you were staying at the Camelot B&B in Schenectady."

Stone shook his head in disgust, but it answered one question that had been bothering me. Wendy had told me Jake still called Clay every day. I knew Jake's real name was Rod but I couldn't think of him that way. To me, he was still Jake Jacoby.

Jake had obviously spoken with Clay and found out Wendy was flying back East to visit Stone and me. Jake had probably had little difficulty in determining Stone and I were the "exterminating" detectives. We'd spoken with his employer, and we were obviously suspicious of his involvement in the murder of Eliza Pitt. With the noose tightening around his neck, I'm sure Jake had gone to the Camelot B&B and slashed the fan belt of my Jeep to the point we couldn't go far before it snapped in two. Stone had noticed a flat tire on his own car that morning as we were pulling away from the curb in the Jeep, I recalled. Jake must have been intent on disabling both vehicles, on the odd chance only one of us went to the airport and drove Stone's Corvette instead of the Jeep.

When Jake called Clay yesterday, Clay had probably told him he was at the airport putting Wendy on a plane to JFK in New York. Jake had gone to the airport, and when we were late arriving to pick Wendy up, as he'd intended, he'd seized the opportunity and abducted her. I was certain now this was the way the events had unfolded. Perhaps Jake had even convinced her he'd come to the airport in our place to pick her up, and she'd voluntarily left with him. Wendy could be too trustful at times, and she was an emotional wreck the last time she'd talked to me, on the phone from the airport. She'd have thought it was odd we'd ask Jake to pick her up, but she might still have gone along with him, regardless, especially since she didn't see us there waiting for her. Wendy knew I'd never intentionally leave her stranded at an airport—under any circumstances—and she may have figured Jake was the only alternative if, for some reason, we couldn't get there ourselves.

We had to contact Clay as soon as possible. Like Detective Glick, I just knew Jake had taken Wendy to the log cabin in the woods that he'd inherited from his foster father. We desperately needed Clay to explain where we could find that cabin.

As if reading my mind, Stone said to Baines, "Jake owns a hunting cabin in the mountains. Do you know where it's located?"

"No. I didn't even know he had one. I didn't know he was a hunter either. I thought his only recreational activity was snorting coke," he replied in an indignant tone. His manner indicated he had a low regard for drug abusers.

Ron turned away from McFarland, but then turned back toward him with one last question. "By the way, what was it you were planning to tell 'Wesson' when you called the NYPD Homicide Division?"

"Oh—uh—just that about once a week or so, an older, white-headed man would come into the club just to speak with Jake. He still does, actually. I saw him in here just the other day. I don't know his name or his connection to Jake. But he pulls Jake off to the side to speak with him privately for a few minutes, and then he leaves. The old guy is probably just a drug dealer.

Probably has nothing to do with your murder case at all," Mc-Farland said, dismissing the importance of the information with a wave of his hand.

TWENTY-FIVE

The four of us were sitting in a small café eating greasy hamburgers for lunch. Stone had called Tufts-New England Medical Center and, after being transferred to a different department several times, he was told Wade Williams had been released three days before. His patient records showed pneumonia as the reason for admittance, and his address was listed as 756 Eighth Street. I recognized the address as Jacoby's.

Stone had ended the call and passed on the information to the rest of us. Before he could reattach his cell phone to his belt clip, another call rang through on it. The caller was Clay, Stone reported as he handed the phone across the table to me.

"Oh, thank God it's you, Clay," I said into the phone. I was breathless in my relief. I never thought I'd be so happy to hear my son-in-law's voice. "Where are you?"

"I just got off a plane at JFK. My connecting flight in Chicago was delayed. Where are you and your friend, er—?"

"Stone Van Patten's his name. Stone and I are in Boston. Detective Ron Glick of the Schenectady homicide division and Stone's nephew Andy are also with us. Right now we're all grabbing a bite at a café across the street from the Fantasy Club."

I'm sure Clay was astonished to learn I'd ever even heard of the Fantasy Club. I knew he was familiar with the place. During our first conversation with McFarland, Baines had mentioned that Clay had picked Jake up at the club at least once.

181

"Did you find Jake there? Have you found Wendy? Is she okay? He didn't hurt her, did he? What's going on?" Clay asked the questions in such rapid succession, he left no opportunity for me to answer them. There was anxiety and concern in his voice. He may have been evasive, and even untruthful, with Wendy, and he may have reacted badly to her pregnancy, but it was obvious to me he did care about what happened to her, and this meant a great deal to me. Wendy had sincerely loved Clay. I would hate to think he could feel complete indifference for her.

"No, Clay. I'm sorry to say we haven't found either Jake or Wendy yet."

"Oh, no." There was a catch in his voice that could not have been faked. "In your voice mail message you said you've found out that Jake is really Rod Crowfoot. How can that be? I never met Crowfoot, but I've seen a photo or two of him. I don't recall him looking at all similar to Jake. How can Rod and Jake be the same person?"

"I don't know, Clay."

"Me neither. But . . . uh . . . well, now that I think about it, if Rod changed his hairstyle, changed from glasses to contacts, and got tattoos and body piercings, it's possible. Like Rod, Jake was pretty puny before he joined the gym and bulked up with the weightlifting. Yes, I think it's very possible, the more I think about it."

"So you think he could have changed his appearance and taken on a new identity after he killed your wife Eliza?"

"Um-hmm. I actually think he could have. It'd make sense to change his identity—especially if he had plans to befriend me. But why would he even want to befriend his victim's husband? None of this makes any sense to me."

"I don't know, either," I said. Clay was thinking out loud, and I didn't want to distract him. I was learning more by listening to his rambling than by asking him questions.

"You know, at the time he approached me at the gym and introduced himself as Jake Jacoby, I had a gut feeling it wasn't just a chance meeting. It seemed orchestrated, almost like it'd been planned in advance. I hadn't known Jake much more than a few days when he offered me a place to stay during the week while I was attending classes at the police academy. I thought he was just a friendly or lonely guy. I still can't understand why he'd want to be near me after he killed my wife. It seems to me it would've been safer and wiser to avoid me. I suspected he was gay, although he never approached me in that way. But he did constantly try to persuade me to break up with Wendy after she and I started dating. He also talked me into selling him my car—"

"And coerced you into doing cocaine with him?"

There was a long stretch of silence before Clay spoke again. Even then, I could tell it was with a great deal of embarrassment that he responded to my question.

"Maybe 'coerce' is not the correct word, Lexie, but, yes, Jake did convince me to try cocaine. And I'm sorry to admit that I really liked it. I was one of those instant addicts you hear about. I know you must be very disappointed in me, and I apologize. It's been tough, but I've succeeded in kicking the habit. I've been clean for a while now, I promise."

"Good for you, Clay," I said with sincerity. "The important thing now is to find Wendy. We think Jake's most likely taken her to his cabin in the mountains."

"Yes, I agree that taking her there would be something he'd do. Jake was very fond of his uncle Bill, the guy who left the cabin to him. Bill was the only foster father he had for any length of time, or at least that's what he told me. He said he lived in a lot of different foster homes when he was a kid, and none of them could handle him. I guess he was bitter and rebellious from being abandoned by his mother and belittled and knocked around by his father. His real father sounded almost as mean and abusive as mine."

As interesting as I found the discussion about Jake's childhood, I knew time was of the essence. The three men sitting around me were staring at me with impatience.

"Clay, can you tell me how to get to Jake's cabin?" I asked, changing the subject back to Jake and Wendy's current whereabouts.

"Yes, I can try, but it's almost impossible to explain over the phone. There's an eagle etching on the door that makes the cabin easy to spot once you get close to it, but getting close to it is an entirely different matter. You have go to the outfitting outpost outside of DeKalb and drive north. Then you turn left at an unusually large, gnarly tree, and turn left again at a sheer rock ledge. You go a ways down a narrow, winding gravel road, then left once more by the old footbridge, before bearing right at a certain fork in the road, and on and on," Clay said. He sighed in frustration. "I know all the landmarks to look for, but I couldn't really describe them to anyone. If you tried to follow my directions, you'd be hopelessly lost before you knew it, I'm afraid."

I was repeating a lot of what Clay told me to Stone, Ron, and Andy. Andy now motioned for me to hand him Stone's cell phone.

"Clay, this is Andy Van Patten, Stone's nephew. I'm helping them try to locate Wendy. We need you here to lead us to that cabin. Listen carefully. You'll need to go to a different gate in another terminal, most likely. I'll have a pilot there, waiting to fly you to an executive airport here in Boston. I'll have to make the arrangements first, and then I'll call you right back with the details. Okay?"

We abandoned what remained of our sandwiches and headed out to our rental car. Andy was talking to his friend named Josh as we pulled away from the curb. Andy had told us that Josh owned a small commuter service in New York City. Andy ended the call to Josh and began to dial Clay's number, which he'd scribbled across the back of his hand. While he waited for the connection, he told us Josh had agreed to shuttle Clay to Boston, where we'd leave the rental car and board Andy's Cessna. Andy would fly the five of us back to Schenectady County Airport. From there we'd all take Glick's squad car to the cabin in the woods. With any luck at all, Jake would be holding Wendy there, and she'd be unharmed when we swarmed in like the cavalry to rescue her. I sent up a prayer that Jake would surrender and hand her over to us peacefully.

As we drove toward the executive airport, I borrowed Stone's phone and called Harriet. I knew she was worried and concerned, and I wanted to keep her abreast of what was happening. I made a mental note for myself that the first thing I'd do when I returned home to Kansas was to buy my own digital cell phone. I'd never realized how handy they were, in general, and how crucial they could be in a crisis.

I leaned back in the seat and took several deep breaths in an attempt to calm my nerves. Although I knew I should be experiencing a sense of relief that things were falling so smoothly into place, I couldn't shake the sense of foreboding I was feeling.

TWENTY-SIX

The Clayton Pitt we picked up at the executive airport in Boston was a different man from the Clayton Pitt I'd known before. Gone was the cockiness and pretentiousness that never failed to get under my skin. An unassuming, timid attitude, and an apparent lack of self-confidence that wouldn't allow Clay to look me in the eye had replaced his old demeanor.

After Clay disembarked from Josh's plane, we all quickly made our way to Andy's plane, still parked in the hangar where we'd left it earlier. Andy shook hands with Josh, as did Ron and Stone, and after we had all expressed our appreciation to the young pilot, we climbed into the small Cessna.

"Anything new to report?" Clay asked once we had taken off and reached our cruising altitude. His question was not addressed to any one of us in particular. It was just a general inquiry that hung in the air for a few seconds before Stone finally responded.

"I don't think we know anything more than you do at this point."

"Oh."

"Can you tell us about how long it takes to get to the cabin from downtown Schenectady?"

"Just over an hour, I'd say."

"That will put us there just before dusk. It's been a long day already, but I don't think we have the option of putting this off until tomorrow, do you Ron?" Stone asked.

"No, I'm not willing to risk it. I want to go straight to the cabin, however long it takes. Clay, tell us about how the cabin is situated. Is there a way to approach it without being detected well in advance? Jake will be armed, I'm sure, and we don't want to put Wendy's life in jeopardy, or be sitting ducks ourselves."

"The cabin sits in a clearing," Clay said. "There's some foliage in the rear of the cabin, but it's not dense like it is in much of the surrounding forest. There are no windows on the north side of the cabin, so if we approach it from that side we shouldn't be as easily detected. We'll want to park behind the timberline though, and sneak in from there, so Jake can't hear the car's engine. There's a rock well on the northwest corner, about fifty feet or so from the cabin. It may offer us some protection if we can get close enough to duck behind it."

"Okay, that's good." Ron said. "The rock well—how big an area are we talking about? Is it big enough for all of us to take cover behind?"

"The well isn't all that big, but there's a rock wall running along beside it that's at least three feet tall, and ten or twelve feet wide. We can all easily crouch behind it."

"Anything else? What kind of weapons might we expect him to have with him?"

"Jake owns a deer rifle that he leaves at the cabin. He also owns a Colt forty-five, a double-action six-shooter. He keeps it loaded and carries it around under the driver's seat of the Mustang."

"Why?" Ron asked.

"According to Jake, it's for protection if a drug deal goes down bad."

"Does he deal?"

"No, but he buys, and uses—a lot. He usually gets his crack, cocaine, and amphetamines from some guy he's known for awhile."

"Who's the guy?"

"Don't know, and never asked. I never met the guy, and Jake never volunteered to introduce us. I tried not to get too involved in that scene. Once in a while Jake would buy it on the street when he was in desperate need of a fix. He bought the Colt after he got his jaw dislocated one night. Owed some dude a bunch of money and couldn't come up with it when the dude tried to collect it from him. The guy sent a couple of his goons to give Jake an attitude adjustment."

"Where did you buy your coke?" Ron asked.

Clay had the decency to look ashamed, but he answered quickly. "It was mostly crack. And I got it all from Jake, although it was only on rare occasions. I was enrolled in the police academy and couldn't afford much at the time, anyway. And I'd have to lay off it whenever I knew it was almost time to piss in the jug. If there was anything predictable about the academy, it was their 'random' drug tests—first Monday, every month, like clockwork. Jake didn't charge me rent to stay at his place, which is why I took him up on his offer. I guess I should have questioned his generosity."

"I would have thought so," Ron said. "But that's past history now."

We all piled into Ron's car and drove to the sheriff's office in DeKalb. Sheriff Crabb was going to follow us out to the cabin. Detective Glick wanted to have at least two armed officers on the scene, and Sheriff Crabb deserved to be involved in the final capture of the murder suspect in a case in his jurisdiction.

When we pulled up to the curb in front of his office, we saw the sheriff sitting in his car, waiting for us. Standing outside his rolled-down window talking to him was Harriet, smoking a cigarette and sharpening a buck knife with a whetstone.

"Harriet!" I yelled out. "What are you doing here?"

If she heard me, she didn't bother to respond. She waved the buck knife at me and jumped into the passenger seat of Sheriff Crabb's car. Stone gave me a questioning glance, and I just shrugged my shoulders at him. One thing we'd both learned in the last few days was that Harriet was unpredictable.

"When I called Harriet, she told me she'd been on the back porch, carving her gigantic pumpkin into a jack-o'-lantern," I said. "She must have brought the carving knife along for protection."

"Reckon her 'pappy' never told her she shouldn't take a knife to a gunfight?" Stone asked, a humorous glint in his eyes.

"Maybe not. Or maybe her 'mudder' told her if she planned to show up someplace uninvited, she shouldn't show up empty-handed." I had returned his playful banter with some of my own, but suddenly his words sunk in and I became alarmed. "Oh, Stone. You don't really think this confrontation will involve gunfire, do you?"

"I think there's a good chance it could result in violence of some kind, Lexie. Jake has a lot to lose at this point. He's apt to go down fighting. That's why I'd like for you to stay behind and let us men handle it. Okay? It's no place for women. You and Harriet would be safer waiting in the car."

"No, it's not okay. I can't speak for Harriet, but this woman is not going to cower in the car while you men risk life and limb to rescue my daughter. I would lay down my life for my child, Stone, and nothing is going to keep me in this car while her safety is in jeopardy. I'm sorry. I really am. But don't waste your breath trying to convince me to stay in the car, 'cause it's just not going to happen."

"Oh, all right," he said in a resigned voice. "Somehow I knew you'd say that. Just promise me you won't try anything risky."

"I can't promise you anything. But it's not in my nature to intentionally place myself in harm's way unless I can see no other alternative. Is that good enough for you?"

"I guess it will have to be." Stone sighed. "I don't imagine I'll fare any better trying to convince Harriet."

On the drive out of town I felt compelled to ask Clay some questions that had been nagging at me. He was open and forthright with his answers.

"How come you never visit your mother anymore?" I asked.

"I do visit her. Every time I'm in town. I call her about once a week too."

Clay sounded sincere and I believed him. Wanda's mental illness must prevent her from acknowledging or remembering her son's attentive devotion to her. I began to doubt anything she had told me was accurate.

"How about your father? Is he in prison?"

Clay snorted, rolled his eyes, and said, "Not that I know of, but he probably should be. My father is a sociopath and is highly delusional. Whenever I was around him in the past, he became hostile and belligerent. When I was growing up, he was abusive to both my mother and me. He's always treated me as if I was some kind of threat to him. After he drove my mother insane, literally, I had to move out on my own to get away from him. I was fifteen. Lied about my age to get into the Navy at sixteen. After about a year, I was tired of living on the streets. I got my GED while I was in the service."

I reached into my purse and pulled out the stack of photos reprinted from the negatives we'd stolen from Jake's house. "Are these your photos, Clay?"

He looked through them briefly and replied affirmatively.

"Is this elderly couple your grandparents? Your mother's parents?"

"No, my grandparents died before I was born. This is the

couple that lives next door to Jake—the Wilsons. Real nice folks," Clay said. "I took this photo of them."

"How about this golden retriever?"

"Yeah, that's Buddy, he was mine. He was a great dog, but he's gone now."

At least Wanda had gotten one thing right. It saddened me that with a disturbed mind like hers, she could identify her son's old dog, but not recognize her own parents.

"Who took this photo of you with the moose at the hunting cabin? Jake? Obviously somebody was with you," I said.

"No," Clay said. He sighed and looked down at his tightly clenched hands resting on his lap. "Actually I took the photo myself. I used the self-timer and set the camera on the hood of my car. The Mustang convertible was still mine at the time."

"You went moose hunting alone?"

"Yeah," he said. Clay sighed again and let his head drop almost to his chest as he admitted having illegally killed the moose. "You don't take a crowd with you when you are poaching a protected species. And you don't offer it up as an alibi either. I lied to the investigators and told them I was studying at the library that day. I realize now that both were stupid decisions on my part. Well, okay—really, really stupid decisions."

Clay glanced over at Detective Glick in anticipation, as if expecting Ron to pull over to the side of the road and slap the cuffs on him. The detective shook his head in disgust, but did not speak. I fell silent myself as we headed up an incline at the base of the mountains.

Soon we began our journey into the forest. Clay gave directions to Detective Glick as we rode along. We'd just passed the sheer rock ledge Clay had mentioned on the phone. The men had been discussing a plan of action, but now as we drew nearer our destination, the air in the car seemed to fill with tension.

Silence prevailed, as we were each absorbed in our own thoughts.

"Over there is the footbridge," Clay said in a near whisper. We were traveling along a narrow gravel road that was predominantly potholes filled with rainwater. Clay pointed straight ahead. "At the next fork in the road we will need to bear to the right. There's a place to pull off the road about a half mile past that. It would be a good place to park the cars. We can walk through the woods from there and come up on the north side of the cabin. That's where we'll be the least visible. And if I know Jake, he'll come out shooting. He's an easily provoked, nervous, and excitable type of guy."

Twenty-Seven

"Ouch!" I whispered before stifling another scream. I could feel stinging nettles on every square inch of my calves. They were pricking me right through my heavy denim jeans.

I'd already stepped into some kind of gopher hole and twisted an ankle and been slapped twice across the face with the backlash of tree limbs. However, the last thing I was going to do was whine and complain about my little aches and pains after being so insistent about not being left behind in the car. I looked up ahead and saw Harriet leading the pack, unconcerned about anything but getting to the cabin as fast as possible. Times a'wasting, I'm sure she was thinking. As I watched Harriet, she reached up, and in one swift motion, severed a dangling limb in two with her knife. As the limb fell to the ground in front of her she leapt over it like a world-class hurdler.

I glanced over at Stone as he slapped at something on his shoulder. It made me think there must be some creepy-crawly thing on me too, so I gave myself a stinging smack on the forearm where I'd recently felt an odd twinge. I suddenly remembered why I'd never been interested in joining a Girl Scout troop. My idea of "roughing it" was when room service was late. Of course, those green uniforms that made any trendy young schoolgirl look like a geek might have figured into my decision too.

"Doing okay?" Stone asked quietly.

"Great. And you?"

"Fine. I can't keep up with Harriet, but then no one else can either. She's a pistol, isn't she?" Stone grinned as he looked up ahead at the sprightly old lady, who was charging through the woods like a rabbit being pursued by a fox. He held out his hand to help me over a fallen tree trunk, ground out a glowing cigarette butt with the heel of his hiking boot, and said, "We'll be fortunate if she doesn't start a forest fire."

I was yanking a tick out from where it had embedded itself in my wrist when we came upon the clearing and the hunting cabin. Stone pulled me over toward him and pointed silently to Jake's white Mustang convertible, parked in front of the log dwelling. Stone made a thumbs-up gesture. This was what we'd hoped to find when we arrived at our destination.

Clay had led us to the clearing and then handed the reins of responsibility over to Detective Glick. Ron was waving to us to follow him, and we were all walking as stealthily as possible to avoid stepping on branches and snapping limbs with our boots. For a moment I thought Ron might make us all drop and do the belly crawl like a platoon of Navy Seals. I was willing to do whatever it took to stay safe and rescue my daughter.

We were less than fifteen feet from the rock wall running alongside the water well when the front door of the cabin opened. Stone picked me up and threw me to the ground behind the rock wall as the whir of a bullet whistled right above our heads.

"Who's out there?" I heard Jake's voice yell out.

Nobody responded. We were all scrambling for position behind the rock wall. A second bullet ricocheted off the front of the old water well. Glick nodded to Clay, prodding him to strike up a conversation with Jake as a distraction.

"Stop shooting, Jake," Clay shouted. "It's me, Clay."

"What are you doing here?" We could hear Jake's voice, but we couldn't see him. The front door with the eagle etched into it was propped open with the toe of Jake's boot, and he was yelling from inside the cabin.

"I'm your friend, remember? I came to see you, Jake. What's going on?"

"You're not my friend, Clay. If you were my friend you wouldn't have left and moved away."

"I had to, Jake, you know that. I had to get away from my memories of Eliza. I remarried, thinking I could block out memories of the past, but even that hasn't helped. You surely understand it wasn't that I was trying to distance myself from you."

I shivered, despite the warmth of my sweatshirt. I had wondered why Clay had remarried so soon after the vicious murder of his first wife. Now I understood he was trying to escape the pain of losing her; much like Stone tried to escape the pain of losing Diana by moving from the home they'd shared for many years. It might explain Clay's reaction to Wendy's pregnancy too. He would have viewed it as a reminder of the child he'd lost when Eliza was killed. I listened as Clay continued trying to calm Jake.

"But it doesn't mean you and I aren't still friends. You knew when you first met me that I was straight."

"I didn't want you in that way, Clay," Jake said in an indignant tone. "I already have a partner in Wade. I just wanted you as a friend. I wanted us to stay close—as buddies."

"We are still close. We talk on the phone nearly every day, don't we? I care about you, Jake. I really do."

"So how come the people I care about all end up leaving me? I'm tired of it. My mother left me, and my father hated me. He put me down constantly until he finally left me. Uncle Bill didn't mean to leave me, but he left me all the same. And then you became my best friend and left me too."

"Is that why you abducted Wendy from the airport, Jake? Was

it to spite me?"

I held my breath as I waited for Jake to respond. After a long silence, Clay spoke again.

"I know you've got Wendy with you, Jake. Why don't you let her go, so you and I can talk? She has nothing to do with this misunderstanding between you and me."

"We can talk just fine with her right here!" There was a loud shuffling noise, and then Jake stepped out onto the front porch with Wendy in front of him. He was using her as a human shield. Her feet were bound together with rope, and her hands were tied behind her back. She looked terrified but unharmed. I breathed a huge sigh of relief. I knew she'd be hurt by Clay's remarks implying that his marriage to her had been a mistake, and I was positive an annulment was in Wendy's future, if she survived this current ordeal. But I couldn't worry about the emotional aspect of this situation now; only the physical aspect mattered at the moment. Getting her out of this unharmed was my first priority. The future would work itself out one way or the other, and I felt Wendy would be better off in the long run if the marriage was annulled. Clay had too many ghosts he needed to exorcise before he settled down with another wife and family.

"What are you planning on doing with her, Jake?" Clay asked.

"I don't know, yet."

"Were you planning to kill her like you killed Eliza?"

This last question Clay threw out convinced me I needed to take defensive action. Jake was obviously deranged and unpredictable. I had noticed that while Jake was listening to Clay and responding to his questions, he wasn't paying much attention to anything else. I pulled away from Stone and did a quasi duck-waddle over to Harriet, crouched down behind the wall. As if she instinctively knew my intentions, she handed me her knife and said, "Watch yer back, sweetie."

Any Navy Seal would have been proud of the belly crawl I

executed to move from the rock wall to the north side of the cabin. I felt like an overgrown crab trying to make its way back to water. Maybe my earlier claim that I was turning into a crab had been prophetic.

As I had edged away from the wall I'd heard Stone start to call out to me and then stop abruptly. I knew he'd been afraid of drawing attention to me. In his heart he had to know the bond between a mother and daughter was too strong to allow me to listen to reason. He seemed to realize his efforts would be better spent in trying to protect me than in trying to dissuade me.

As I inched along the side of the building with my back flush up against the logs, I heard Clay shout out. I could tell he was choking back tears as he spoke. "Why'd you do it, Jake? You didn't even know me then. So, why did you have to kill Eliza?"

I was now peering around the edge of the building, trying to think of a way to distract Jake. He was swinging the gun around wildly. Up closer now, I could tell he was definitely under the influence of drugs. His eyes were red-rimmed and glassy. His movements were jerky, and his reactions were slow and uncoordinated. I was afraid the gun would accidentally discharge from his careless handling of it.

"I didn't kill Eliza!" he said, swinging the gun from side to side.

"Yes, you did! Admit it, Jake!"

"I didn't kill her, Clay. I swear I didn't! He did—" Jake said, pointing at the door with his gun, as it swung open again and a stout, white-haired man walked out on the porch and ducked behind Jake and Wendy. His complexion was so pale that he'd have looked like an albino if not for his light green eyes. "I just brought Eliza to him when he asked me to. It was Uncle Ho—"

"Dad!" Clay hollered in disbelief.

"—mer. Uncle Homer killed her, not me."

"Dad, what are you doing here?" Clay asked. His voice had risen several octaves in his hysteria. "Jake, what are you doing with my father? What's going on here?"

"I met him outside a crack house in downtown Boston one night. Homer's been like a father to me ever since. When I lost my uncle Bill, I felt like I was alone in the world. But then I met Homer. I'd do anything for him now. He may have been your father at one time, Clay, but now he's mine. He's kind of adopted me as a foster son. He told me you disowned him as your father, and that you'd pay dearly for doing that. He even told me I could call him 'Uncle Homer' and—"

"Shut up, boy!" Homer said. "You've said more than enough already."

"And 'cept for Uncle Bill, Uncle Homer's the only one who—"

"I said put a sock in it, boy! Don't you know when to keep your damn mouth shut?"

As Homer turned and backhanded Jake across the back of his head, he noticed me peeking around the corner of the house. He grabbed the Colt .45 from Jake's hand and fired a quick shot in my direction. He missed his target, and I fell backward into a thorny bush. Detective Glick hollered at me to stay down. He stood up and fired a shot back to the right of the threesome huddled together on the porch. He couldn't risk firing a shot any closer because Wendy was positioned in front of the two men. I think Ron just wanted to advertise the fact he also had a firearm he was ready and willing to use.

Homer returned fire with two wild shots back in Glick's direction. I flinched when Ron grabbed his arm as he ducked back down behind the wall.

That was the fifth shot to come out of Jake's Colt .45. By my recollection. Clay had said it was a double-action six-shooter. I hadn't noticed Jake take the time to load new bullets into the revolving cylinder. Homer now had possession of Jake's gun, and he had just one more unspent bullet. I'd have to come up with a way to make him waste it.

"Hey Jake!" I shouted from my position, flat on my butt in the bush. I knew my backside would look like that of a baby hedgehog's. I could feel numerous thorns embedded there, but with the adrenaline speeding through my veins, I was impervious to the pain.

"What?" he hollered back with a defensive edge to his voice.

"How come you let Homer talk to you that way?" I asked.

"What way?"

"Like you're a half-wit who can't think or speak for yourself. I'd say he's just using you as a pawn in his evil game. Bet he'd stand back and let you take the rap for him too, Jake. Seems to me like he treats you with even less respect than your real father did."

"No, he don't. He's always been good to me."

"Gives you cocaine when you need it, things like that?" I asked.

"Uh-huh. When I need it."

"Oh, so is that how he controls you, Jake? He buys your loyalty by supplying you with drugs for your habit? A habit you are finding hard to finance, isn't that right? He knows your weakness, and he takes advantage of it and uses it to get you to do his dirty work for him. He doesn't care about you, Rod, he's just using you, manipulating you. Deep down, you know that's true, don't you, Rod?"

I had intentionally switched to his real name to jolt him back to reality.

"Well, maybe a little—"

"Oh, yes, I can see why he's so special to you, Rod. Why can't you see that he's evil, and when he gets taken down— which he will—he'll take you down with him?"

"Oh, but, he's uh—he only killed Eliza to teach Clay a lesson."

Homer backhanded Jake again. I couldn't see them but I heard Homer's hand make contact with the back of Jake's head and the bones in Jake's neck crack as it snapped forward from the force of the blow.

"Ow!" Jake exclaimed.

"Shut the hell up, boy! You really are a half-wit, aren't you?"

"Hey! Don't talk to me that way!" Jake said. He pointed my way and continued, "She's right, you're starting to talk to me worse than my real father. I did everything you asked me to do, and now look at the way you're treating me, like I don't mean a thing to you. No wonder Clay's been avoiding you all these years."

I was beginning to understand how badly Jake's childhood had affected him. Between the emotional scars of the past, and the drugs of the present, Jake was a very vulnerable and confused young man. He'd be easy pickings for a vile and manipulative character like Homer Pitt. Apparently, Homer was using Jake to enact vengeance on his son, Clayton. Clay had commented earlier that his father was a mean and abusive man. He was worse than Clay had imagined. Not only was he not "Father of the Year," he was also a drug dealer, a kidnapper, and a murderer.

If Wanda had been correct that Homer had been redheaded, his hair had probably just naturally turned white since she or Clay had last seen him.

Jake had completely forgotten about Wendy. He had stepped away from her to confront Homer. Homer was pointing the Colt at Jake. His stark white face was now pink, flushed in anger. "Quit your whining, you ninny. You're no better than that no-account son of mine who thinks he's too good for the likes of me, his own father. I wasn't worthy of his love and respect—

and now I'm not worthy of yours? Ha! Well, I showed him! And I'll show you too, you little two-bit redneck."

A shot went off a split second before I heard Jake scream and fall to the ground. That was the sixth shot, I thought to myself—the final round was spent. This was my chance. Without a second thought I jumped up onto the porch, wailing like a banshee, with Harriet's buck knife raised high in the air. Homer stepped back in alarm at my display of pure madness. He fell over backward in his haste to get away from the menacing-looking weapon I was brandishing. He knew from my reckless behavior I would not hesitate to use it on him. I'm sure I must have resembled something in a scene from a *Friday the 13th* movie.

Then everything happened at once. The events that followed were a symphony of sights, sounds, smells, and feelings, colliding into each other as all of my senses came alive. Each observation imprinted itself on my memory and would remain stored there indefinitely. It was as if the next few minutes had occurred in slow motion.

I remember Wendy's eyes appearing as large as teacup saucers as she stared at me in shock. Jake was lying across the threshold of the door, clutching his wounded shoulder. I could smell his warm blood running down the crevices of the eagle etching on the door. "Click, click, click," I heard, as Homer lay on his back and fired at me with a gun that had run out of ammunition. Detective Glick, Sheriff Crabb, Clay, Stone, Andy, and Harriet were storming the front porch and tackling Homer. I saw Clay rear back and smash a fist into Homer's face. I heard bones crunch and saw blood stream down from Homer's nose. I saw Detective Glick show me an indentation on his arm where he'd been grazed by Homer's bullet, when he saw my shocked stare at the bloodstain on his shirtsleeve.

I felt Sheriff Crabb take the buck knife gently out of my hand

and cut the ropes that had been binding Wendy's arms and legs. Wendy and I both had tears in our eyes as we embraced in grateful relief. She whispered into my ear, "Homer told me he was Stone when I got off the plane. Jake must have told him Mr. Van Patten's name. I'd never met either of them, Mom, so I believed him. I'm sorry."

"Honey, it's not your fault," I assured her. I comforted her as best I could. I knew the heartache was just beginning for her. Clay came up behind me, and I walked away so he could embrace her too. I heard him apologize for deceiving her as he had. He told her he'd come to realize he'd need counseling before he settled down with a wife and family. She agreed with a resolve that amazed and relieved me.

I then turned around and saw Ron slap a pair of handcuffs on Homer and another pair on Jake. I smelled cigarette smoke as Harriet lit up a Pall Mall behind me. I heard Andy call 9-1-1 on his cell phone. Finally, I felt Stone pull me to his chest and embrace me tightly. I heard him say, "Oh, thank God you're okay. I love you, Lexie. Don't ever do anything that impulsive and courageous again."

"What did you say, Stone?"

"I said you are one crazy, impetuous, utterly adorable woman."

"And?"

"And if you do ever do something like that again, I'm not sure my heart will be able to handle it. It almost stopped beating when I saw you jump up on the porch. It hadn't dawned on me yet that you'd realized the gun was out of ammo. After the dust settles, how about if we spend a few days traveling up to Maine and New Hampshire, so you can really see the beautiful fall colors?"

I didn't get him to say those three magic words again that day. Even so, I knew he loved me and I loved him too. I readily agreed to a trip to New England with Stone—just the two of us, getting to know each other better. I decided I was ready to take the next step in our relationship, and I told him so. I couldn't just drive home to Kansas and forget him. That would be impossible at this stage.

"Ah, so I'm beginning to grow on you a little?" Stone asked.

"A little." I teased.

"Kind of like Harriet's coffee?"

"Yes," I agreed, laughing. "Exactly like that!"

ABOUT THE AUTHOR

Jeanne Glidewell, a 2006 pancreas and kidney transplant recipient, and her husband, Robert, reside in the small Kansas town of Bonner Springs. Prior to moving back home to Kansas they owned a large RV Park in Cheyenne, Wyoming. Besides writing, she enjoys fishing, gardening, and wildlife photography. Jeanne has published numerous magazine articles and is a regular contributing staff writer for *County Magazine,* a Distinctive Media Inc. publication based in Lansing, Kansas. Her second Lexie Starr novel is titled *The Extinguished Guest,* and she has also written a mainstream fictional novel. She's a member of Sisters-in-Crime and Mystery Writers of America and is currently working on the third novel of her Lexie Starr cozy series.